BLOODMOON

"Megan? Are you okay?"

"I'm fine. This is so like you, letting someone else do the dirty work."

"What are you talking about?"

"Your friend got here an hour ago, told me you couldn't get away, and helped me move everything in."

"What friend?" Ken grew silent for a moment. "Megan, listen to me. Where is he now?"

She noted the intensity of his silence.

"He's sitting next to Lauren. They're getting along—"

"If you can get away, do it. If not, don't let on anything's wrong, and I'll be there right away." Ken's tone was urgent, yet filled with love and a promise. "I won't let him hurt you, Megan. I love you."

She could barely speak.

"I'm scared, Ken."

"I know, baby. I'll be right there." He was quiet, firm, his firmness most reassuring.

"Don't hang up," Megan pleaded.

"Let me call Lauren."

All Ken heard next was a loud scream and an even louder, "Mommy!" followed by a taunting, "Come for me, Ken. I'm waiting in the Forge. By the way, it's just us now, no one else. Just you two," the killer warned, looking at Megan and Lauren, "or they're dead."

BLOODMOON

BY

CARTER JOHNSON

Adapted from the screenplay by Keith
Strandberg

Commonwealth
Publications

A Commonwealth Publications Paperback
BLOODMOON

This edition published 1996
by Commonwealth Publications
9764 - 45th Avenue,
Edmonton, AB, CANADA T6E 5C5
All rights reserved
Copyright © 1995 by Carter Johnson

ISBN: 1-55197-889-X

Designed by: Federico Caceres
Photo Stills from the Major Motion Picture
BLOODMOON supplied by: Keith Strandberg

Printed in Canada

SEACONAL FILM COPERATION and MEDIAS present
BLOODMOON a NG SEE YUEN & KEITH STRANDBERG
production
Associate Producers KOSIT SUVINIJJIT
YUWADEE BOONKRONG
Production Advisor Prof. CHAROEN WATTANASIN
Production Supervision PAIROJ ASVADHARES
Starring GARY DANIELS CHUCK JEFFREYS
DARREN SHAHLAVI NINAN REPETA
Special Apprance by FRANK GORSHIN
Co-Starring JEFF PILLARS BRANDIE ROCCI
LEIGH JONES JOE HESS JEN SUNG OUTHERBRIDGE
Screenplay by KEITH W. STRANDBERG
Music by RICHARD YUEN Edited by ALAN POON
Director of photography DEREK M.K. WAN
Action Choreographer TONY LEUNG
Art director JOHN TING
Producer KEITH W. STRANDBERG
Executive Producer NG SEE YUEN Director TONY LEUNG

To Carol, Karen and Evan.

Chapter One

A quick jab. His sparring partner flew backward. A fast left, a cross to his partner's chin. So quick, Chavez didn't have a second to react. He was in the ropes, breathless, his gloves flying up to protect his face.

From the corner, cauliflower-eared Hobbs, who'd been relishing the rapid spitfire action of his young champ all evening, turned to the other boxers punching speed bags around the ring.

"Damn, he's quick! He's still got it!"

Overhead, just above the gym's ancient, splintered and splintering door, hung the banner "Home of the Light Heavyweight Champion of the World." Hobbs pointed to the banner as if the others working out in his gym didn't know who was sparring in the ring. A rush of pride, the result of years and years of hard work, ran up and down his spine, into his withered hand, across his face. He grinned. He felt great. Fifteen, sixteen years yelling and demanding, barking and coaching in this falling-apart room had turned into something: Eddie Cunningham was *the* Light Heavyweight Champion of the World. Now and for a very long time to come. And he was his.

Chavez came off the ropes, determined. Cunningham belted him in the stomach. Twice. So fast that Chavez would later argue he was belted "once." A sucker punch from Cunningham. Chavez backed off. A second and he was spitting, prancing forward, managing to throw a tight-fisted punch. Connecting, slamming Cunningham's head backward. Pain shot across his forehead, jabbed his brain behind his eyes, fueling Cunningham back into even faster action. Jab-jab-right uppercut! Chavez was back in the ropes.

Hobbs felt it, knew it. His champ was still in top form. There would be more fights. Maybe Vegas, certainly Atlantic City. Top venues. Top money. A year or two, he'd be outta here. He and the Champ. Living like they never lived before. Well deserved.

The bell rang, and Chavez, exhausted, slumped to the ring's floor. Eddie headed toward his coach, ready to go another five-six rounds with yet another sparring partner. "Bring 'im on! Get 'im in the ring. I'm ready, Ernie!"

The manager-trainer-corner man shook his head, tapped his watch.

But Cunningham was energized. "I'm working the bag, Ernie."

"Closing time," Hobbs scowled.

"You go on." Eddie bent down and under, stepping through the ropes. "I'll lock up."

Hobbs shrugged his shoulders. No sense trying to change his champ's mind. "Tomorrow then," he said as he was moving out the door.

"Count on it," Cunningham grinned, throwing a punch in the air toward his going-home coach, trainer, handler, everything-man.

Within ten minutes, the gym emptied out. Most of the lights went out, and Cunningham moved to the heavy bag hanging near the ring.

He began punching. Throwing a right. Bouncing a left off the bag. Blam, *Blam*! The thick heavy bag swung backward, sailing into the dented wall. Sweat ran down his face, rivers of salt, down from his pits, down his bare sides. He was hot, triumphant.

And winded.

His arms ached. Stressed burning muscles screamed for relief from the continuous night-long work-out. He'd pushed himself tonight. He was ready for more fights. He was on top and would stay on top. "Bring 'im on!" his mind shouting and seeing the bag fly backward, smacking against the wall three feet away, punch-after-punch, goaded him, like a waving cape to a snorting bull, to keep going, to keep punching, ignore the burn. Grueling work-outs made the ref's holding his arm high up in the ring, spitting into the microphone, "Ladies and gentlemen, in a knock-out in the first round—Light Heavyweight Champion of the World Eddie Cunningham, the winner!"—and hearing the crowd roar all the more sweet.

Snap!

The sudden sound caught Cunningham off-guard. Pulled him back from Madison Square Garden to Hobbs' dingy second-floor gym.

He turned toward the door, half expecting to see Hobbs shuffling in, barking, "Call it quits!" for the night, pissing and moaning, "Gonna wear yourself out!"

He saw no one.

The door was closed, yet the deadbolt's bar was shoved in place, locked. How could Ernie have—?

Cunningham looked around the room. No one. He stepped toward the ring. No one. He crossed to the iron-barred window overlooking the Lower East Side. Except for an almost full moon, redder than usual, shining in, no one.

He shrugged off the strange, eerie feeling someone had actually entered the gym. He moved back to the heavy bag, still swinging back and forth, back and forth, its rusty chain creaking as it swung. He focused himself and his sagging energies back on punching the bag.

He forced his paining, resisting arms to slam the oblong piece of stuffed leather again. Again. Again. In his mind, each punch to the bag was a cross to Salvo's head, an uppercut to Diveccio's stomach, a pounding on that runt Puerto Rican the promoters wanted to slate against him next ("What! A champion going up against some new-comer hardly in the ring, what five, six times? KO'd twice! Is this some kind of high-roller's joke?").

"You fight well." The words came from out of nowhere. "Champ." Or was his body so tired his head was going off, his senses playing tricks on him?

Snap.

Cunningham turned. Squinted. Someone had to be there.

No one. Nothing.

"But you don't," he heard from out of the hallway that led to what passed for a locker/changing room, "have the killer instinct."

"What the hell?" Cunningham strained to see as the lights suddenly went out. The gym went black. A second later—snap—and a single bulb hanging overhead the ring went on. "Who—?"

"I can show that killer instinct to you." Someone was standing in the ring. He was tall, bare-chested, the physique of a man who was disciplined and worked, every day, by some hard-ass trainer. He wore black sweats and flame red boxing gloves. His leer beneath long shiny black hair challenged Eddie to enter the ring as he sneered, "Champ."

"Is that a fact?" Cunningham didn't move, not a step. "Well, maybe some time we could go a round or two."

"No time like the present." The stranger indicated the empty ring, then glanced at the moon shining through the window. He looked at Cunningham. "Or are you scared?"

Cunningham's eyes did a quick look-see, up and down this stranger's body, his mind instantly calculating, evaluating. This leering prick had more weight on him and from the length of his arms, a reach advantage. Yet Cunningham's strength lie in his speed. He worked his combinations so fast most opponents thought a jab-jab-hook was one punch. Another jab-jab-hook to the head, a jab-jab-hook to the stomach, and his opponent went down, flat on the canvas! Barely hearing the ref's, "Eight—nine—" and slap to the canvas, "TEN!" So, thinking he'd played this stranger's game, whatever it was, Cunningham stepped into the ring, making eye contact with the stranger, grinning a friendly, "Lucky I still have my gloves on."

"Did you notice," the heavy-booted stranger averted his eyes from Cunningham's to the window after the Champ stepped into the ring, "there's blood on the moon tonight?"

Cunningham turned to look. Quickly, the stranger was on top of him, an iron pipe slammed into his kidneys.

Caught totally off-guard, in fiery, excruciating pain, Cunningham doubled over. A right uppercut and Cunningham's head flew backward. Air exploded out of his nostrils and sweat flew into the air.

A slamming cross to his chin, to his stomach, to his head, quicker than he could react. A slam to his head split open his temple.

Stunned, Eddie went down.

"Key to winning is to take advantage of every weakness," the stranger sneered. Eddie was gasping for breath. "Like how you never quite—" as if to demonstrate his lesson, the stranger snap kicked Cunningham's back, spun and sidekicked his kidneys, leaped and sent the ball of his foot driving into the side of Eddie's neck "cover your side, Champ." The stranger's heel slammed into Eddie's clavicle, into his lower abdomen, hard into his groin.

Fire exploded inside the champ's chest, shot up his neck, rammed into his brain. His head spun; his mind went black; he gasped for air. Blood and sweat running into his eyes, down his cheek, he struggled to get back up, to stand to his feet, his arms hung limp, all but refusing to work.

"Always attack," a crashing strike to Eddie's kidneys, another to his forehead, and another, working the bleeding cut, "is lesson two." Eddie's head guard flew off. His blood smeared the stranger's glove.

The stranger pounded Cunningham's forehead again and again, enjoying the sound of the clenched glove's thwacking impact on Cunningham's temple, time-after-time, splitting flesh, punch-after-punch, sending blood flying into the air.

In fiery pain, Cunningham fought to come back against this stranger. A jab connected with the stranger's ribs. A right blocked the stranger's left hook. Struggling for breath, his legs becoming watery, blood from his temple running into his mouth, he stepped toward the stranger and was powerfully mowed down by the stranger's right leg whipping low and out.

Cunningham fell, cut down. The stranger spun, leaped onto the fallen champ, eager to kick and pound every inch of Eddie's flesh, especially his bloodied head. "Hey, man,"

Cunningham's tired, stinging hands crawled up to hide his face from the stranger's maniacal pounding, "enough."

"It's never enough!" the stranger spewed, continuing pounding. Cunningham's head. His neck. His windpipe. Kicking Cunningham's ribs. Jabbing Eddie's temple. Working the bleeding areas. Again and again. Slamming his fist into the Champ's stomach, lecturing. "Lesson three: a true champion never goes out easy! Never lets up." He hammered the Champ's solar plexus and sent a flying kick to the base of Eddie's neck.

Eddie flew upward, then thudded to the canvas, his breaths long and hard in coming, his thud throwing gasoline to the stranger's already raging, "Fight! Dammit! Fight!" The stranger screamed.

His foot slammed into Cunningham's groin as if the Champ's balls were his to punt, at will, for the final winning point.

Cunningham's mouth flew open to scream. No sound. Another quick punt! Cunningham didn't move, never felt it. The stranger kicked and punched, kicked and punched, long after there was no movement.

And would be no movement. More kicks. More punches.

The stranger clamped Cunningham's limp head between his bloody, red gloves. He held Eddie's head steady as he focused on the Champ's swelling face, the hollow, staring eyes. He felt deep disgust at the lack of real challenge from this "Light Heavyweight Champion of the World." He punted one final punt: Eddie's chin, quick, fast, hard, with all his might. The boot ripping into Eddie's skin, shooting Eddie's head upward, backward.

The champ slammed into the ropes, clunked to the canvas.

"School's out, Champ." The stranger spat, really pissed his student hadn't hung around to complete the lesson.

Chapter 2

Detective Burke slid his classic racing green Triumph motorcyclebetween two cruisers, braked, and parked.

Yellow crime scene plastic tape was everywhere, keeping the cops in, the press and gawkers out. Even at dawn, reporters were clustered around an irritated Chief Hutchins, out-shouting each other, "Is it the work of the same killer?" "Got any suspects?" "Any communication from the killer?" "What's going on here, the police won't cooperate with us?" "Tell us something!"

"Okay," Hutchins sneered, "Why aren't you guys out humping your ladies at this hour, 'stead of me?" Pissed, he walked away from the screaming mob and into the building that housed Hobbs' grungy gym, just as Burke stooped under the yellow tape and without any exchange with the chief hurried through the door, taking the steps two at a time toward the second-floor gym.

"What do we have here, ladies?" Burke asked, striding over to two shields standing guard over someone who no longer needed such protection. "Talk to me, girls. Talk to me."

"One dead boxer," one of the shields answered. "Eddie Cunningham, 33, Light Heavyweight Champion of the World."

Burke squatted down, eyed the boxer he had twice seen KO some up and coming unknown at the Garden. Admired his style. Fast. Real fast. Apparently this time not fast enough. "Took quite a beating," he said to no one and himself.

"Found in the ring an hour ago," the other shield offered, "by his trainer-slash-manager. Pretty broken up, his manager." The shield indicated Hobbs, who was seated on a long wooden bench, painted peeling green, along the far wall. Hobbs was just staring into space as if he wasn't there. "Hasn't said much, if anything, since we got here."

Burke looked at Cunningham's head, eyes swollen shut, dried, caked blood in the sockets, along the purpled lips, all up and down the neck. Huge bruises on each side of the head, under the chin.

Burke glanced up at the shields, "Our boy? Make this five?" as he ran a long silk white scarf through his closed fist, pulling out a blue scarf, a red scarf, a blue scarf, one of his incessant magic tricks. A habit that drove Chief Hutchins up a wall!

"No witnesses, no finger prints, Cunningham's blood's everywhere. On the ropes, smeared all over the floor of the ring. Perp must have grabbed the Champ's head and rolled it back and forth and around on the ring's floor."

"What the hell kind of guy is this?" The pulled scarf returned to its former white color.

"Enjoys killing," from the one shield.

"Or making sure his victim's dead," from the other.

"Where's that M.E.'s report?" Burke stormed to his

secretary as he entered his cubbyhole office. "He wasn't in his damn four floors down office."

Margie, used to her boss's constant demands without an acknowledgment of her presence after all the years, added insult to injury, "Chief's on two. He's been holding for you a good ten minutes this time."

Burke sauntered into his office and picked up the phone, stating, "I'm working it, Chief," before Hutchins had a moment's chance to chew out his ass. Too late!

"We need answers, Burke! Now! Damn press was all over me this morning. Have you read the papers? Seen that damn Kim Hunter running her mouth all over TV?" Hutchins was furious, fuming.

Burke tried to interrupt, "Chief, I'm—"

Impossible.

"What're you doing on this one?" Hutchins roared. "Taking a year-long shit on public time? Stop fucking around and—"

"Came in last night, Detective," Wallace said, entering Burke's office, a file folder in his hand. "Before the boxer."

Burke put down the phone—the chief still loudly ragging him out—and took the folder. Opening it, he saw a computer print-out. A graphic. A large full moon, flame red. Blood dropping onto a caption: "Blood on the Moon."

"Shit!" he muttered as he turned to the wall bulletin board, already crammed with other computer print-out messages. Each message more brazenly challenged his investigative abilities or taunted his skills or screwed with his mind, deriding his person. "Who was it sent to?"

"Attached to e-mail addressed to the chief."

Burke pinned the graphic next to the other print-outs. For a moment, he studied the graphic, the first of its kind. Only written messages before this full moon, dropping blood. He looked from message-to-message. "Catching pussy more important than catching killers?"

"Up yours, Burke. I'm getting closer. You're not."

"You bleed the same color as me, honkey."

"What the fuck're you doing? Answer me!" The phone blared.

But Burke had no answers. Not on this one.

～・

"Outta here, you shit!" Dutch kicked the wino out of his place. It was a few minutes past two a.m., and Dutch Schultz, long-haired, greasy, tired and all sweaty from tending bar with no relief for more'n twelve hours, was shutting down his place.

His place was little more than a dank, smelly hole in a basement wall in this run-down section of the Lower East Side. This hole passed for a bar, but was actually a meeting place for pimps and their aging, fattening whores. Here, money was exchanged for schedules, dates, times, and places, an occasional beating when needed.

Dutch didn't pay much attention to those who frequented his place or why. Long as nobody bothered him and they dropped a few dollars his way, what went down in his place, he could care less. That way, he didn't know shit whenever the cops came by looking for somebody or expecting him to sing, something he was ("I know my rights!") constitutionally against. That and he knew he'd get his ass and face kicked in if he ever spilled what he knew.

Then again, to keep his face and ass from getting

kicked in by the damn, friggin' cops, he'd sing all right. And long. But not the tune or the words the cops wanted. So now everybody pretty much left him alone, and he left them alone. And every night was more of the same: shoveling winos and most every night two-three of his regulars out the door when he wanted to close up or ball Roxy.

Tonight it was Roxy.

Her tight butt swished from side-to-side as she kept slipping quarters down the guzzling juke box, pushing trucker song buttons, fantasizing her thin, silky-red, K-Mart on sale, made in some third world country by el cheapo labor panties were being pulled down by massive long-haulers. They pulled her panties down slowly and very tantalizingly, teasing her thighs with their big, thick fingers. Moving closer. Closer. Then a fast rip, and they were off! And they were barreling down her road with a job to do.

Oh, yeah.

She'd worked her share of truck stops, but nowadays, "No more." After ten years, doing everything herself, including some on the side pimping, she'd had her fill of smelly, tóo-small restrooms, trying to put her cranberry delight lipstick on looking into mirrors cracked in four pieces or none at all, being laid on truck seats, her rump almost always, every damn time, being pushed into the stick shift sooner or later 'cause the long-hauler was usually so big he couldn't maneuver his huge roly-poly stomach mass unless she scooted on her side and gave him as much room as possible. As she said before and she'll tell anyone again, just ask, "No more!" Dutch might not be the most romantic; in fact, he wasn't at all. He might be immense; she felt crushed every time he was on top of her, always more certain this would be the time her lungs would give way under the flaccid pressure bearing down on her and she'd stop breathing. He might not bring her to pleasure every time; in fact, most often, he was done and all over and she hadn't even begun. But Dutch was steady. He was here and came every day. He didn't have a wife to lie about. No kids. And he kept her in what she needed and gave her what she wanted. A wad either way.

His fat hands grabbed her butt, slowing its thumpin' back-and-forth swishing. She giggled. He squeezed, and she wriggled. Backward, into him. She giggled again. Even more giggling when he sucked on her neck. "Ooh, Dutch!" He-he-he.

Dutch pulled Roxy more tightly against himself, always lovin' the prickling feel of growing harder, filling, poking through, once, twice, finally big enough to tumble out of his boxers, all while still in his pants.

Instinctively, Roxy reached behind her, her hand cupping his growing, which took a sudden quick upward hop at her touch. She giggled like a school girl the first time. She loved making his hooter hop!

Dutch pulled her around to face him. He grabbed and pulling open her blouse. He buried his scuzzy bearded face between her breasts.

She pushed her breasts hard up against his lips. His hands kept moving around and under her shirt-covered butt. In one quick upward movement, he hoisted her up onto the pool table across from the juke box. Three balls went rolling out from underneath her. Now firmly seated, about to be laid down, she pushed her breasts against Dutch again, harder this time, while she reached for his fly. She was like a long-hauler's dispatcher urging delivery sooner, faster than expected.

Dutch moved slightly, making her hand's entrance

into his wetted boxers easier, quicker please! She stroked him, up, down, up, down. He moaned, "Yes, yes, more." Twirled her fingers and played in the hair that engulfed his organ, lightly tip-toeing around and under, about to grab. His entire groin and lower abdomen tightened, shivered, jumped, eager to pump. He was com—

Snap.

She zipped her hand out of his boxers.

"What was that?"

"Nothing, Roxy, nothing," pulling her back up against him again, hungering, alive with prickling desire, unable to hold—

She scooched back, off him. "No, Dutch, I heard something."

"Me coming," Dutch snickered. He pushed his lips back into her luscious treasures, sucking her hardened nipples, a child with a snow cone, loudly. "Nobody messes with me and mine," he growled moving from one mound of hot ice to the other.

Snap.

"Somebody's here!" She wriggled, pulling herself out from under his sloppy fat. "I don't want anybody watching." She struggled to pull her bra up, her blouse closed. He hadn't gotten into her panties yet. One consolation if she was being watched.

She moved toward the door to the outside, angering Dutch.

"Get back here, bitch!" he scrambled to pull up his pants and hurry after her. "Roxy! Roxy! Get back here! Roxy! We're—"

The unsatisfied gadfly moved quickly behind the bar, grabbing a bottle just in case someone was inside, watching, all the while mumbling, complaining to herself, "My luck with men is for shit."

"Roxy," his voice was very smooth, very sexy, inviting, coming from where? "Your luck is about to change."

Taken by surprise, she turned, "Huh? Who—?" In a flash, his hands slid around her neck, squeezed. Her hands flew up to grab his which tightened vice-like and twisted quickly, expertly. Her breathing stopped momentarily; she blacked out. He grinned as she slid against his body down to the floor. With his heavy-booted foot, he rolled her behind the bar.

"Find anything, babe?" Dutch was still hard, still struggling to move.

"She found me, Crutch."

"Huh?" Dutch's first impression was "the place is locked. Nobody's in here," but for some reason, he spit out, "The name's 'Dutch'."

"Not after tonight."

"Who the fuck?" Dutch, his swelled organ going limp immediately, stared at the tall man, bronzed, long-haired, leering down at him, disgustedly eyeing his giant girth, a sneer beginning to etch its way across his perfectly-sculpted, thick Middle Eastern lips.

The fifth of Roxy's six trucker tunes flipped into place. Its wailing notes blared from the jukebox.

"Great night for a dance," the stranger tittered, moving toward Dutch, almost imitating Roxy's incessant sexually-tinged giggle.

"Who the fuck are you? How'd you get in here?" Dutch protested the intruder's advancing steps. "The place is closed."

The stranger's leer changed to a "too bad" look as he kept moving toward the fatty bartender-owner.

Dutch grabbed a chair and shoved it between himself and the intruder.

The chair hit the intruder in the knee. He feigned being hurt, as if he wanted to back off.

Dutch grabbed a half-empty Coors bottle from off a table. He smashed it against the table. The bottle shattered, and he held in his hand a sharp, jagged weapon. Dutch rammed the broken bottle toward the intruder. The stranger again backed off, purposely letting himself slip on the foamy beer on the floor that had spit out of the Coors bottle when it broke.

Seeing his chance, Dutch was on top of the intruder, confident he could jam the jagged Coors into this fucking intruder's olive fucking face.

"Can we talk this over?" The intruder seemed frightened, scared, as if getting more than he had bargained for. The intruder pled. "Really, Crutch, let's talk."

"No way." Dutch spit in the intruder's face. His lips curling up over his blackened teeth in a sneer. He'd show this intruder who was boss in this hole.

"Please," barely audible from the intruder's simpering throat.

"You're mine, fucker," Dutch laughed.

WHAM!

The intruder's foot shot straight up! Sharp lightning slamming into Dutch's back.

Dutch gasped, shocked. He whammed the bottle down toward the intruder's head, hard. The intruder rolled, arched his back, sprang to his feet. His fist rammed into Dutch's giant stomach. Again. Again. A third time. A ball of iron sledge-hammering Dutch's wobbling belly.

In seconds, the intruder slammed the wind out of Dutch.

Dutch slumped over, zoning out.

Thwack! The intruder back-handed his fist into the

base of Dutch's neck. Thwack! Thwack!

Fiery pain shot in all directions through Dutch's sagging body.

"Why don't you fight better," the intruder hollered, "*Chump*?" slamming his foot into Dutch's neck, into his windpipe. "Huh, Crutch?"

The stranger jammed his rock-hard knuckles into Dutch's eyes, turning, twisting. Searing pain shot through Dutch's skull, the stone ring on the stranger's gouging middle finger cutting into the bar owner's eyelids. Water and blood oozed into Dutch's eye sockets, running down his cheek into the long, ugly hairs of his unkempt, almost never trimmed beard.

Dutch screamed in torment. Disgusted at the lack of challenge, the intruder grabbed Dutch's head, yanking, twisting, inflicting more and more pain. A second later, skillfully thrusting his thumb and right index finger into both sides of Dutch's throat, his thumb and finger pinching the windpipe shut. Twisting and pulling Dutch's flesh outward, downward in one fast, quick jerk.

One last choking desperate gasp for air from Dutch.

Then nothing.

The intruder kicked the huge lump of leaden flesh with all his might, as with the Light Heavyweight Champ of the World, disgusted Dutch hadn't put up a better fight.

Then he left. Out into the night. Glad he hadn't wasted more time in that hole.

Chapter 3

Ten years in working in various Manhattan emergency rooms, including a two-year (much too long!) stint in the Bedford-Stuyvesant human trash pit, night-after-night, plus a three years in the psych ward at Bellevue before a lateral move to NYPD, Lower East Side, and the city's morgue, from all over the city, had prepared Medical Examiner Horton for almost anything. He'd stitched every cut everywhere on the body, removed every foreign object imaginable from every body orifice that existed, identified burn victims with little left but a bridge or a crown, but he had to admit to Burke, standing next to him beside the huge hardening naked body, "I've never seen wounds like this."

Burke could barely even look at the man identified as #456 by a wire marker twisted around the man's chubby big toe. Massive purple abrasions, frozen, hardened by death, covered his much of his body, especially the upper chest area, neck and head.

Horton continued, "Killed by trauma to the head. His extremities," Horton pointed to what looked like swollen purple pouches and were once hands, feet, "the bones were shattered."

Burke cringed while Horton stated the obvious, "This one died in extreme pain. The killer has a knowledge of anatomy. His destruction is systematic, precise." ME Horton pointed to the temple, the windpipe, the kidneys, "Every strike is to a vital area, a nerve center or a meridian. He definitely has a signature. I recognize it," Horton continued, pointing out what even Burke could tell for himself was excessive force.

"Any evidence of a weapon?" Burke asked. "Or post-mortem mutilation?"

"No, to both." Horton was rather clinical in answering now, adding, "It doesn't look like he used a weapon. No punctures, no cuts, but—tell you the truth, Detective—in my years in this city, I've never seen wounds like these." Again pointing to the chest, neck and kidney areas. "And once they're dead," he seemed certain, though not one hundred percent, "he's done."

"What about the witness?"

"Killer choked her out before she could see him clearly," Horton was back to sounding clinical. "Didn't hurt her. I have her looking at mug shots anyway."

Outside Dutch's place, Kim Hunter stood, in a can't wait mood, microphone in hand, nevertheless having to wait for her cameraman's signal. She perfunctorily smoothed her smart-looking powder blue pin-stripped suit, quickly wet her lips with her tongue, more a habit than needful, and in her mind practiced her lead.

5—4—3—the wired cameraman's fingers counted down—2—1—and "You're on," he pointed.

"Very early this morning, police were called to this Lower East Side pub by neighbors saying they heard 'unusual noises' during the night. Police arrived to find forty-two-year-old Dutch Schultz lying bludgeoned to death on the concrete floor of his establishment. Schultz' girlfriend, Roxy Schwertner, was also found unconscious.

"A quick examination at the scene by City Coroner Ribbinkof revealed the pub owner was beaten to death. Nothing was ransacked. The cash register was still closed. Police on the scene said at first glance robbery didn't appear to be the motive.

"Police Chief Hutchins declined to be interviewed and would not confirm whether or not this was the work of the same killer believed to have recently murdered five other local individuals. Sources inside the police department would, however, say the beating that killed Schultz was consistent with the manner in which the five others were murdered.

"No arrests have been made in this or the previous five murders. Police Chief Hutchins also refused to comment on whether these murders were the work of one killer, possibly—but not necessarily—a serial killer. For more, we go to Greg Houser at Police Headquarters."

Kim's camera went black as master control back at WGSN cut away to an iso of Greg interviewing District Attorney Nels Guren.

"Wantta go inside, Kim?" her cameraman asked.

She shrugged. "For what?"

"Collateral footage for the noon report."

"Leave that for the dailies," she said, snapping off her mike. "I'd rather catch an interview with Hutchins."

"Won't happen, Kim," the cameraman was breaking down his tripod, packing up his lenses. "Ask me, that cop's afraid of something."

"Getting booted from his job maybe?" Kim said, more as a statement than as a question. "If you ask me, he's taking a powder on this one."

"Doesn't mean they don't have anything on what's been happening." The cameraman was a bit defensive of the man he'd worked for as NYPD crime scene photographer for a semester as a college intern. "Remember, the Unabomber took how many years?"

"Yeah, but that was going on nationwide. This is one city." Kim was down on Hutchins. He had a miserable, actually embarrassing record promoting women officers. In fact, he'd been forced by the mayor to hire more women or hit the streets. So, not wanting to lose 55K a year plus benefits and a whopping big health insurance plan for himself and family, he'd hired more women—twenty, in fact, at one hiring—then forgot them, letting them walk the same beats year after year while their male partners advanced almost every review period up the ranks and, as follows, up the pay scales. Kim knew this for a fact. Her mother was one of those twenty hired by Hutchins.

"Okay. Let's drive over to police headquarters and grill his ass on camera." The cameraman suggested.

"Nah," Kim vetoed his idea, thinking of her mother still walking a Lower East Side beat.

"I'm assigning you some help in this, Chuck," Hutchins was definite, no backing down. "I want you to go see this guy."

"I don't need any help, Chief," Chuck balked.

"We have six dead bodies, a techno-freak nutball who sends computer messages about the murders, and we're no closer to solving this than we were on day one." Chief Hutchins circled his detective as if drawing the noose tighter. "Did I forget something?"

The Chief scratched his head, making a show of suddenly remembering what he hadn't really forgotten.

"Oh, yes, the killings are getting closer together. Not a good sign." Hutchins sounded like a teacher lecturing a beginner student.

"Chief—" Chuck balked again. Feeling put down actually.

"You need to shut up, Chuck." The Chief's eyes narrowed, his tone sharpened. "And let me tell you something. Get some results on this one or—"

"I'm working my ass off!" Chuck was insistent. "The Great Chucker can book himself magic shows in Atlantic City 'cause he won't be working here!"

Chuck clammed up. At least he knew when he was being told off.

That and he needed the job. To keep up his support payments or his ex'd be hotter than the chief was! He pocketed the magic trick, the spongy red ball he was about to pull out of Hutchins' purple-red-veined nose. This was not the time.

"I've got heat from everywhere on this one," Hutchins was yelling now, his reddening face betraying the fact he was close to losing it, "and I'm trying to stop the bleeding! Get Ken O'Hara. He specialized in serials before you got here. He was one of the best mindhunters in the country. Retired a couple of years ago."

"Mindhunter?" The look of bewilderment magnified Chuck's consternation with his boss. "What the hell is a mindhunter?"

The Chief didn't bother to explain a mindhunter's a serial killer chaser. "Beginner," he sneered under his breath, then pressed a slip of department paper into Chuck's hand. "Here's his address. His last serial was a messy one. Put O'Hara in the hospital, almost put him six feet under."

"I don't need any help." Chuck didn't even look at

the paper.

"Yeah, and I'm not going to need a triple bypass one day. Go see O'Hara. I want him on this." Hutchins' tone now told Chuck the chief had reached the point of no return. "And, Chuck, wear a suit. Try to make a good first impression."

The Chief showed his detective the door.

The conversation was over. So'd be Chuck's career as a detective for the NYPD if he didn't hustle his buns...toward O'Hara.

Chuck left Hutchins' office. Two steps later, cursing "Shit!" under his breath, he read the slip of paper.

Chapter 4

"Can't we stay longer?" Lauren was insistent, really, really hoping, her blue eyes begging. "Just one more day?" Excitedly she added, certain this would get him, "Tomorrow, we can go diving in the waves!"

"Wish we could, Lauren," came the answer, from his heart, honestly. "I really do." Thirty-two-year-old Ken O'Hara, rugged, muscled, actually quite impressive in his skin-tight muscle shirt and shorts, looked down into his blonde seven-year-old's begging eyes, "But you know the rules."

She grabbed his hand and squeezed while begging, "Please, daddy, please!", a technique that almost always succeeded in turning ex-cop and martial arts expert O'Hara into Mr. Softy. "Pretty please." Her excitement at being with her father at the shore showing in her big, eager, one tooth-missing smile as she ran and pranced along the boardwalk, still clutching his hand and with everything in her, pulling this massive hunk toward the boardwalk's wooden railing and, thus, closer, closer to the sparkling, sandy beach.

Less than a foot away from the stairs leading down to the white sand, having let himself be dragged (actually helping a bit!) clear across the boardwalk from the salt water taffy store, Ken planted his sandaled feet against the wooden walkway and dug in! That sudden stop ended Lauren's excited prancing/pulling toward the beach. She slipped backward.

"Come on, Daddy!" she turned, pleaded.

"We can't, Lauren," Ken tried his hardest to be firm. "It's getting too late this afternoon to go into the water."

"There's lots of people in the water," thinking her father meant the beach closed at a specific time and pointing toward the hundreds and hundreds of sunbathers and surfers having a grand time, "See!"

"Not for them. It's getting too late for us." Reluctantly admitting, "I gotta get you back home."

"Let's call in sick." Lauren tried a new tactic, something she'd seen on a TV show recently.

"What?"

Sensing success, at least trying for it again, the towhead plopped down on the boardwalk. She quickly left go of his hand because she now needed both of her hands to prop up her drooping, dizzy head. She rolled her eyes and let her tongue slide out from between her lips. She slobbered a bit as her head drooped lower and lower, almost to her knees. She coughed. She choked. She bleated, "I'm sick, Daddy," barely getting out the words. "Real, real sick." She was doing a fairly good imitation of the physical actions and sappy dialogue of the grown-up actress who had used this ploy to con her boyfriend into staying longer and, among other things, vacuuming the rugs! It had worked on TV, but Lauren was getting the impression real life wasn't imitating TV. Not this time.

Ken didn't move, didn't even bend down to nuzzle

the pride of his life. Instead, firmly, knowingly, "Won't work, sugar. Your mommy'll suspect right off."

Her dad was right, of course. Like he always was. If he brought her home even five minutes after the agreed-upon time, her mother went ballistic. Thought her daughter had been kidnapped by her father! Or something terrible had happened! Or—whatever the most horrible tragedy her mind could imagine at that hysterical moment! And always—when he brought her home, safe and sound, and more importantly, deliriously happy—always, she threatened to sue his pants off! Adding, shouting, "I'll move away! You'll never see Lauren again!" "Please, Daddy," Lauren looked up at her sandy-haired 6' 3" father now towering over her and knew she couldn't change his mind, not on staying at the shore another day, but maybe, she begged, "Couldn't we change the rules?"

Ken knelt down beside his daughter, looking into her eyes, his hand tenderly brushing away the several tears welling up in her eyes, and wondered what he could tell her, being honest, yet not tearing down her mother in her eyes.

For her mother, his wife, being married to him had been a constant battle to overcome fear and, worse, anxiety attacks. Almost since day one. They'd been teenager sweethearts, he and Megan, meeting on the home gridiron one Friday night their high school sophomore year when he was a starting quarterback (as a sophomore!) and she was featured in the routines of their school's cheerleading squad. Both were quite the handsome athletes, beyond their years, actually. And very popular. Physically developing and accomplishing athletic feats much earlier than others. And relishing their accomplishments.

And each other!

Yet even back then, she'd watch him get banged up, tromped and stomped on, bruised and ending up at the bottom of some pile-up so often during each game, she'd begin worrying his head would be affected. And absolutely certain his head was as she watched him game-after-game waiting 'til the very last second to throw the ball, then aggressively—recklessly to her—charging into the line, openly seeking knock-down, hitting action. Later that night he'd say, like he said after every game when they were together, "Everything for victory!" Then she'd cry, "But what'll be left for me, you get hit so often?"

He'd heard it so often he began getting even more aggressive on the field, knowing she'd be watching, worrying. But, oh, later that night, the warm cuddling his faint-hearted apology would bring. That made getting stomped to a pulp and enduring her worry worth it!

Then there was the night he'd told her he was planning to go away to the police academy for training as an under-cover cop. She went completely berserk, totally hysterical, screaming, hollering, "Why? Why? Why? Some pusher somewhere'll find you. One shot and you're dead!"

"But, Megan," he pleaded, "I want to help get the trash off the streets."

"That'll never happen," she wailed. "They'll kill you. They'll kill you," she kept repeating over and over and over, his arms around her, holding her against himself tight, offering no comfort, changing nothing. "They'll kill you. They'll kill you."

And that night there was no cuddling. No response to his gentle nudges.

Finally, through the six years of their marriage, afraid to answer the phone when he wasn't home late at night, afraid *if* she answered of what some cop she'd never met would tell her, afraid to know when he was working undercover or commandeering a raid or drug bust, even more afraid whenever he put on his kevlar vest before leaving home, she just couldn't take it. Her knowing he thrived on his work, that he got spiritually high believing what he was doing really mattered in the community, knowing any of this didn't make his leaving the house any night any less stressful, even knowing he'd leave her with a whopping insurance settlement, meant nothing. She wanted him close to her at night. She wanted him beside her as they watched their only daughter grow up. All her growing-up years! She wanted to laugh at his pathetic jokes and feel absolutely tingly all over whenever he came up behind her, put his arms around her and began kissing her neck. She wanted him, she wanted Ken, not some memory, not some piece of paper from a funeral home, not some medal from the NYPD.

Ken or nothing.

But he couldn't understand that. Or, if the truth be known, wouldn't.

Her fears turned into constant nagging. Which led to daily petty bickering. Only easing up the days, the nights he didn't go into work for whatever reason. The bickering intensified into verbal fights, then open hostility.

Much too often in front of Lauren.

It was obvious. To both Megan and Ken. For the sake of their mutual sanity, he'd have to give up police work.

Or she'd have to leave.

She made the choice. Taking Lauren with her.

"Your mommy wouldn't like that too much," he admitted the truth, something they both knew and now lived with once a week during their times together.

"Why can't Mommy understand?" She climbed into his open arms, putting both her hands around his neck, hugging and hanging on, for dear life.

He hugged back, glad her head was over his shoulder so she couldn't see the tear forming in his eye, and at the same time seeing his wife in his mind, her look of contempt every time he brought their beautiful child home, even more so if Lauren was smiling and laughing and holding onto his hand as the two of them skipped up the steps to the front porch together. He said very quietly, tenderly, actually, to Lauren, "I don't know."

They hugged each other for what seemed like forever, only broken by Ken's cheery, "How about some ice cream, Sugar?"

And then they were off, walking hand-in-hand down the half-century-old boardwalk. They hurried toward "Arnold's Scoop," their favorite hang-out whenever they just absolutely had to have cookies and cream in a waffle cone topped with sprinkles, sometimes peanuts, almost always a cherry!

"What'll it be today, young lady?" mustachioed Arnold, giant dipper in hand, slid open the plastic top of the ice cream cabinet. "Rum raisin, mocha cream?"

"C'mon, Arnold! My little girl's only seven!" retired detective O'Hara joshed the ice cream vendor he'd known for more than ten years, ever since he'd worked day-and-night for three months, doing the impossible and what no one else at the department could or was able to do, tracking down the stalker who raped and knifed the ice cream man's college freshman daughter. With little to go on, the other detectives had given up, satisfied to file away the meager available data about the rapist until he struck again. Maybe that next time, the victim'd have a bit more information, and added to what the police already knew, the rapist could be tied to Arnold's daughter.

Apprehended, tried and sent up the river.

But Arnold, an ice cream man at the Jersey shore all his life, specializing in smiles and friendly exchanges with his customers as he handed each a cone, a sundae or a shake, begged Detective O'Hara to find the man responsible for violating his daughter, making her afraid to walk on the streets, anytime, making her fearful of men, turning his once smiley, chatty daughter Kathy into a paranoid homebound shadow of herself, existing in misery.

The sight of his pained daughter grieved Arnold deeply. Sickened him, actually. "I'll get my own damn militia! We'll go after the prick!" he shouted into Ken's face.

Ken had remained silent.

"I don't got much," Arnold yelled, "but I'll buy as many thugs as I can. I'll finish that fucking prick off! I'll feed his dick to the sharks! After I've chopped it off myself!"

When Arnold could think of nothing else to do to the prick, Ken quietly assured the man, "I'll find him. I'll Bring him to justice."

"Justice! I don't want justice!" Arnold hollered. "I want my daughter back!"

There was almost no description from his daughter. It was a few minutes after ten on a Tuesday night during the fall semester. She was walking back to her dorm from the library across campus after three hours' research for some semester-long project (she couldn't even remember now what project she was working on; she never finished the project; she never went back to classes) when she was pulled down behind a large clump of bushes. Then pushed and dragged, a knife in her ribs, toward the student parking lot. There, she was slammed up against a foreign car's hood, hard, her head yanked back and held back so all she could see was the cloudy night's murky dark skies above her.

But she could remember his hand, the hand not yanking and holding back her head, reaching up under her sweater, clawing, grabbing.

She had tried to scream. She couldn't or didn't remember feeling the knife. Only her bra giving way, exposing her breasts. Later, she'd remember hearing him lick his lips as he cupped her breast in his hand. She tightened every muscle in her body, angering him. She tried to push him off. He slammed her up against the car's hood again, even harder.

She struggled, trying to get her leg up high enough to knee him. He yanked her head back again so hard she thought she heard a cracking, twisting. Then she went under, never remembering being shoved into the car, never remembering his forced entrance, being knifed and cut, carried from the car and placed behind a dumpster. Never remembering the ambulance speeding her to Our Lady of Mercy Hospital.

Only weeks later, almost a month, after reliving the whole experience over and over in her mind; and again, tonight just before getting into bed, over and over in her mind; while trying to fall asleep, over and over in her mind; tomorrow while getting up, looking out the window, over and over in her mind; a terrifying memory constantly replaying, rewinding-replaying, only after weeks of this nauseating terror was she able to give Detective . O'Hara two very scant notions. Not so much memories; more impressions from her senses, which she didn't know whether or not she even could trust. The hand that had cupped and pulled and squeezed her breast was rough, very rough. His skin she meant. And he smelled of oil or gas or something you'd put into a car.

The others on the force were quick to jump on maintenance men working at the college. Rough hands, automotive smell, easy first conclusion. But two weeks of investigations yielded a brick wall. All ten of the college's maintenance staff anywhere near the college that week could account for their whereabouts that evening. Each had air-tight alibis, witnesses to boot. Also, the maintenance staff was a graying, paunch-expanding lot that maybe could have pulled her down, then pushed and dragged and slammed her up against a car's hood, then yanked and felt and grabbed and squeezed, then fended off her kick to his groin, violently yanking, pushing, and twisting her back down onto the car's hood. Yeah, they might have been about to do that, all of that. But if they had, they surely wouldn't have had enough left to get it up yet!

So, the others wrote their reports, filed their folders under "Open," grabbed their ticket books, and went back out on the beat, checking red-flagged parking meters, waving to children, and doing what their chief wanted: being jovial with and being seen in the community. Always PR in the community.

Not O'Hara.

He staked out the college, three and four days and nights at a time. His boyish good looks, an almost buzz haircut, a build perfected by years of pumping, running and disciplined eating, he looked more like a college tight end or mid-sized grappler than the ten-year police officer he was.

Night-after-night, he hung out. This dive, that little pizza pub, over at Hooly's Hole where on Monday nights all the beer you could swill was "Only $2, Forget the tax!" And he talked. Endlessly. About calculus classes, biology labs, and the crappy girls this college had to offer. He was going to transfer, going to go somewhere where a "D" meant more than a grade. He complained. About Professor Erker's flirtations with his graduate assistant secretary who also happened to be his student and the unfair reading assignments Erker expected: 50 pages a night, which his assistant/secretary/student never seemed to have read. About the most recent hike in tuition and the decline in quality of the professors at this educational factory! About the prick-teasing girls here, always teasing, always wearing necklines so low a guy got a hard on fast and hurting just looking, then—"Shit! Don't they always these days?"—demanding rubbers at the most inopportune times, when in another moment, you'd explode, "Why doesn't the cunt know how we can't just up and stop the train when it's coming?" but now—"Damn. I'm not HIV-positive! What's she got to worry?"—now, you've got to fumble around before re-entry, and then—"after all this, you don't satisfy her just right, she's ready to claim you took advantage of her!" And they're all like this around here! "You know what I mean?"

"Yeah, law's gotta be changed!" he'd said after O'Hara'd spewed out the same invective five nights in a row to a hundred different guys. "When're these girls around here ever gonna just shut up and take what they want anyway without bitching at a guy before, during and after?"

"Man, if it's like that for you, bitching 'before, during and after, pal," O'Hara swallowed another gulp of Bud, looking into the kid's eyes, "why even go balling?"

"Gotta get something outta life," the kid shot back. "Sliding under cars all day, shovin' mufflers up the engine's ass, well, hell, there's gotta be something more to a day than that. Know what I mean?"

O'Hara grunted. "Yeah." He swallowed another gulp, wiping the foamy run-off from his lips. "What'd ya do all day that makes bitching while you're balling worth it?"

The kid pointed to his sweat-stained T-shirt, snickering, "Read my pecs."

The words "Mickey's Quickies" stretched out across his chest. "Lubes and mufflers in a minute" peeked from underneath his breasts. "Up your car's in a flash" crawled across his lower belly. "Name's Mike," the kid offered, sticking out his hand, "if you ever need a body job of any kind."

O'Hara shook Mike's hand. It was callused, full of hardened ridges.

"Your work close to here?"

"Five minute walk," Mike said. "Boss figures he can pick up a lot of the commuter trade. You know. Have their car serviced while their brain's being filled."

"Your hours? During the week." Ken was suddenly sounding like a student with car problems.

"Seven to nine," Mike answered, trying to be a helpful bud, then confiding, "Don't get outta there most nights 'til 9:30, though. Then it's over here for a beer or whatever else gets my mind off shoving metal up against metal all day long."

"Think I'll stop around," Ken said, extending his hand again, shaking Mike's. "Maybe next week." He made a mental note of Mike's appearance. "Later."

"Yeah, later," then a quick, "Boss gives students like

you a good deal," as Ken was moving away from the bar, toward the door. "He won't stick it to ya like a lot of other garages do."

An hour later, Ken was sitting on a bench across the street from Hooly's Hole. Playing a hunch. Just waiting. It was almost 11. He'd been hacking around this campus since seven this morning. His bed was beckoning. Surely Megan had already spent an hour worrying and fretting. His ass was gonna get chewed out again tonight. Yet, the thought of Arnold's daughter—NO! TRUTH! Why couldn't he admit it to himself?—the thought of his daughter being jumped by a horny slug like "Quickie Mickey's" Mike kept him on the bench, waiting, playing a hunch, wanting to wretch as he imagined what Mike thought of all day as he "shoved mufflers up engines asses."

Around midnight, Hooly's Hole emptied out. Mike was among those exiting in a group, laughing, slapping some obviously-drunk guy on the back. O'Hara's eyes followed the mechanic. Mike walked to the student parking lot, unlocked and got into an Oldsmobile Cutlass Cierra and drove off.

Damn.

For two weeks, O'Hara made it his business to hang around Hooly's Hole about 10, closer to 11, wait and watch. Finally, he saw what he already suspected.

Mike walked toward a dorm. Near the dorm's entrance, he pushed himself through a clump of bushes along the dorm's wall. O'Hara moved closer. He heard the sound of Mike relieving himself.

About ten minutes later, a female was walking toward the dorm. Mike's hand reached out, grabbed the girl, pulled her back into the bushes. In seconds, Ken was on top of him!

"Such a pretty girl for only seven!" Arnold swooned, rolling his bushy eye-browed eyes. "So, what'll it be, Miss O'Hara?"

"Cookies and cream!" Lauren squealed. She pointed to the round box that held her all-time favorite, the same flavor she pointed to every time at "Arnold's Scoop."

"Coming right up!" Arnold fairly sang, twirling the dipper in the air and swooping down into the brown ice cream bucket, gouging out a giant scoop filled with lots of crispy cookie bits, which he plopped into the waffle cone, all in a matter of seconds.

Lauren reached upward as high as she could for the cone. She pressed herself close to the ice cream cabinet and went up on her toes, trying to get even a few inches higher.

Teasing her gently, grinning, Arnold held the filled cone a bit higher. Lauren tried to go up on her tippy toes even higher. And as she went up higher, the cone went up higher, an unattainable delight.

Determined, Lauren tried to climb up the ice cream cabinet, only to slide down its shiny metal surface. Frustrated, she turned to her burly father, and before she could ask, "Help, Daddy," he slid his hands under her arms and hoisted her upward toward the cone. Just as Arnold pushed the cone downward toward her, laughingly making a loud, snorting bull-dozer sound plowing the air.

It was a game. It was always a game. Two men very, very glad they had their daughters in hand.

Suddenly, the cone almost in her face, Lauren pulled back, her quick backward action throwing her father off-balance. Ken stepped backward, out onto the boardwalk, bumping into a college student, a babe and a beer in his hands. The beer spilled, its foam shooting over his bare chest and swim trunks. Wetting the front of his neon-orange trunks as if he'd suddenly had an accident. The beer fell to the walkway.

Pointing to his darkening crotch, the girl laughed. The student, his fist tightening, spun around toward Ken.

"Sorry, man!" Ken said quickly. "It was an accident."

"Really!" the babe pointed to several wet dribble spots down the middle of the guy 's trunks. She laughed. "Looks like you pissed yourself!"

The girl's hooting turned the student red. He moved toward Ken, growling, "You're gonna be an accident!" He threw a punch toward Ken's head.

Ken's hands flew up to protect Lauren, still in his arms, as he stepped back to avoid the student's second punch. "Hey, man, it was an accident. Let me pay to clean your trunks. Twenty dollars do it?"

The student's foot flew up, a quick flick toward Lauren's head. The child screamed as the student shouted, "I'll take it out on your hide!"

Clutching Lauren more tightly, Ken whirled around, deposited the child on the ice cream cabinet's counter, nodded quickly to Arnold, whose hands encircled the frightened child, and turned toward the student.

"Look, I said I was sorry."

The student, his eyes inflamed, threw another punch, which Ken sidestepped. "Hitting me won't dry your trunks."

The girl admired Ken's cool. Why didn't she ever meet someone like him before she met cocky bodybuilders whose brains were stuffed down their jocks. She eyed this student's groin. Even wet, there wasn't much to see. Not even the thinnest outline of anything. Imagining a little link sausage, she laughed.

"Yeah, asshole!" the student sneered, hearing the

babe's laughing, pissed by her looking down there at him. She was putting him down. He could feel it in her eyes. In self-defense, he tightened his fist, taking a step closer toward Ken, now almost in his face, spitting, "But it'll make me feel a hell of a lot better."

The student swung. His tight fist, an iron ball, slammed into Ken's temple. Lauren screamed, "No, Daddy! No, Daddy! Did he hurt you, Daddy?" as swing after swing, the student pounded Ken's head, then a solid punch to the ex-cop's stomach.

"Daddy, leave him alone!" Lauren screamed. Arnold dropped the cone into the strawberry marshmallow container and tightened his grasp around his friend's only child. Arnold had seen Ken in action.

Only once before. But that had been enough to convince him. Ken was no man's fool.

"Why don't you fight back, pussy?" the student growled, throwing a high kick toward Ken's neck. Ken ducked, rolled, falling to the ground.

The student jumped toward the rolling Ken. His arm flew backward. Suddenly meeting a tugging resistance! The student whirled around, finding himself facing an angry Lauren who had pulled herself from Arnold's grasp, jumped off the ice cream counter, ran toward the bully and was now pummeling him. Trying to, anyway. Wanting to protect her father, not thinking of any consequences other than not letting this mean man stomp her daddy, she was now pulling on the student's arm.

The student raised an open hand to slap Lauren off him!

Instantly, Ken was up, flying through the air, a roundhouse and flying kick into the student's back. The student flew forward, landing face down on the boardwalk. His nose smacking downward between two wooden slats.

Ken grabbed Lauren, assuring her, "He can't hurt me!" He put his daughter back on the ice cream counter. Arnold pulled her behind the counter.

Just as the student sprung up. Leaping toward Ken, who spun around, a high kick to the student's shoulders. The student flew backward, then, swearing, "You motherfucker!", charged Ken, whirling, kicking and cursing.

Ken eyed the student. Embarrassed rage drove the kid. He was out of control.

He was about to defeat himself.

The student slammed his foot into Ken's chest, hard, kicking again and again, like a powered air hammer slamming against cement. Ken side-stepped each kick a second before the student's foot would have pounded into his chest.

A quick turn and Ken grabbed the student's shoulders. Pulling him backward. Powerfully throwing him into the wooden corner wall of "Arnold's Scoop." The student's trunks suddenly got wetter. The babe laughed louder, and the student, his eyes breathing fire, leaped toward Ken, who punished the student's persistent insolent arrogance. A kick to the knees. A fist to the stomach. A lightning-fast foot slam to the student's hairless chest, knocking the wind out of the student, who dropped, unable to take the beating he himself had provoked. The student choked, gasping for air. Ken moved toward him, a fist ready to end the choking. The student's hand flew upward, a desperate sign signaling, "Enough!"

The student crawled away as fast as his hurting knees would take him. To the accompaniment of the frizzy babe's laughter.

Ken shrugged his shoulders at the retreating cou-

ple, then turned toward Lauren, no longer hiding behind the ice cream cabinet. She was out front of the ice
cream shop jumping up and down, clapping and cheering.

Ken walked to his daughter, extended his arms. She
jumped, and he hefted her up.

"Sorry you had to see that, honey," Ken said quietly, cradling Lauren against him. "You okay?"

She looked into his eyes, felt his strength, saw his
love, "Are you?"

Ken grinned. "Yeah."

"Why'd you fight him, Daddy?" Lauren's pride
sounding now like concern.

Ken became serious. His arms instinctively tightened around his child. He spoke quietly. "He was going
to hit you, Lauren. I had no choice." Then, more to himself than to his daughter, "Nobody hurts my family."

"Hey, you guys!" Arnold called out. "Still want
these?" He held two new cookies 'n cream waffle cones
in his hands.

"You bet!"

Chapter 5

"He's dead!"

"Dead?" Chuck's heart skipped a beat. He wasn't prepared to hear that. What should he say? Why didn't Chief Hutchins know that? Why send him all the way across town, over the bridge, all that traffic, and half-way out the island if mindhunter O'Hara was no longer among the living? He stumbled to say something meaningful, "I thought—" and got cut off immediately!

"When he gets back with my daughter, our daughter," Megan fumed, correcting herself, "he's going to be!"

"I see." Now Chuck really didn't know what to say. "Uh, you guys divorced?"

"Separated. Not good." She snapped through the front porch screen door. "It's his afternoon with Lauren. He's late! I hate it when he's late."

"I was hoping to find him here," Chuck offered a quick reason for his presence. "Business."

Megan eyed the rather handsome guy whose one arm he was holding behind his back. Hmm, strange.

Why? Didn't look like a salesman. No briefcase, no portfolio. Unless that was what was behind his back. Didn't exactly look like a sheriff or sheriff's deputy about to serve divorce papers. What sheriff rides a— hmm, what kind of cycle is that parked along the curb? She looked at the man and realized he was struggling to find the right words to say to her at this moment. Her heart softened a bit toward this man who was standing, obviously a bit taken aback by her attitude. She smiled.

"I'm Megan" she said as she pushed open the door, extending her hand, into which Chuck quickly placed a bouquet of pink and yellow flowers, a gesture Hutchins had suggested as a way to softening Ken's almost certain initial negative response. Obviously the chief wasn't up on the latest between Ken and Megan.

Suddenly finding flowers in her hand from this stranger so startled Megan that she stepped through the door, accidentally stumbling down the step from the door to the porch. He caught her, and they both laughed, just as Ken drove up in his Honda with Lauren.

"Who's Mommy with?" Lauren turned to her father as he brought the car to a stop.

Ken's answer was a look of disapproval as he watched his wife pulling herself out of the stranger's arms, then straightening out her dress, flowers in her hand.

"Where have you been?" Megan demanded immediately when Ken got not even half-way up the walkway.

"We were having fun," Ken sounded defensive to Chuck, who found himself the brunt of Ken's scowl, "if that means anything to you. Right, Lauren?"

Lauren ran toward her mother, happily, excitedly shouting, "Mommy, you should have seen—"

"Not now, honey," Megan curtly cut off her daughter. "We have an appointment."

Ken eyed Chuck suspiciously.

"I bet you do," slipped out under his breath.

"You promised to have Lauren back on time," Megan was steamed.

"Now I'm late. Say 'good-bye' to your father, Lauren," Megan demanded.

No cordialities, no hug, no hint or explanation who the stranger was in whose arms she had just been for how long? If he hadn't driven up just then, where would they have been next? And flowers? Who did this stranger think he was? They were still married, he and Megan. Separated didn't mean open call for his wife. Not to him.

Reluctantly, Lauren saddled back to her father. She touched his hand. He bent down and hugged her. "See you soon, babe!" kissing her lightly on the cheek.

"Love you," Lauren kissed him back, "Superman."

"Right back at you." Ken winked and hugged his smiling child again.

Megan pulled the house door shut, not thinking, quite from habit, but Ken took the gesture personally, especially with this stranger standing there, as a message to him: "Stay outta my life." She took Lauren by the hand, and without another word to either Ken or this stranger, walked straight to her car parked along the curb, Chuck's flowers still in her hand.

Ken opened the house door. Chuck didn't move.

"Lost your way, huh?" Ken said to the tall stranger. "Hit the road."

"Came to see you, Ken," Chuck sounded determined.

"Yeah, well, nothing personal." He watched Megan

and Lauren pull away from the curb. "But fuck off!" He walked through the doorway and entered his house.

"Chief Hutchins sent me to see you." Chuck sounded even more determined. "With this." He held out the serial killer file folder.

The name "Hutchins" stopped O'Hara, abruptly. *No*, he thought immediately. His eyes saw the file this stranger held out toward him. "Not interested," he said.

"That's what the chief said you'd say." Chuck didn't budge from his determination. "But he wants your help." He pushed the file toward O'Hara, almost into his gut. "Just have a look."

"No." The answer came firmly, without hesitation, as he moved to close the door.

"Chief said you quit over a case. That right?" Chuck's tone was almost demeaning. He still held the folder out toward Ken. "Just have a look," he repeated, deftly, matter-of-factly.

For reasons he'd never know, actually almost a learned response from years of the force, Ken reached out and took the file, though spitting out rather unceremoniously, "Give my regards to Hutch." Another learned response. And then he was gone, inside his house, behind the closed door, leaving Chuck standing outside, thanking the chief for adding this irritating impossibility to his life. On the other hand, O'Hara had the file. Mission accomplished.

Burke got on his Triumph and rode back to the station. As he drove all the way back across half the island, over the bridge, and into the Lower East Side, his mind replayed the case. Almost nothing to go on except the killer's signature: excessive force spewed on his victims. That and the taunting computer messages. And that damned bloodmoon.

He wasn't much of a cook. Growing up, he was mostly into the martial arts. Actually, if he could have done it, he would have existed on liquids, power-packing vitamins and some fruit.

So, waiting for the water to boil to cook a pack of frozen butter beans for dinner—at least he could do simple culinary tasks like that, and he hated to nuke 'em, hated the taste and maybe the off-chance nuking added a touch of radiation he didn't want—Ken stood beside the stove watching the water, waiting, and opened the file folder.

Inside were black-and-whites of Eddie Cunningham and Dutch Schultz, lying beaten to a pulp where they were found. His stomach tightened. He closed the folder, threw it on the kitchen table and returned to tending the boiling water, lightly tossing the frozen chunk, his dinner, into the bubbling water. He watched the bubbling water but saw the brutality inflicted upon Cunningham and Schultz.

During his bean dinner, he opened the file again. Why? Habit? Learned response? Something nagging inside him? Could he help someone?

He spot-read the police reports. The champion boxer and the bar owner were the latest two of six murder victims. Because of the violence common to all six, the department was calling this a serial.

Ken closed the file. He wasn't going back. No matter how many pictures Hutch sent over! Or strangers bearing bouquets of flowers for his wife!

At 10, Ken hit the shower. He slipped out of his shorts, pulled off his tank top, then his boxers. He couldn't help seeing his back in the floor-length mirror Megan had mounted on the wall a week or so after they were married. She always was checking something. Her hem line. Her hair. Her butt, especially whenever she was bemoaning the fact of the additional twenty-plus pounds that "camped out" on her hips after Lauren's birth. Megan always referred to added pounds as "weight camping out," her way of fooling herself that, after a while, the weight having enjoyed its reason for being there—in this case, pregnancy—it would pack up and go south! To this day, she was still waiting for the weight to vacate the premises.

The mirror showed Ken the huge deep purple scars that criss-crossed his upper back. Reminded him every time: a butcher knife was slashing through his back, ripping through his taut skin, tearing into his muscles, pain searing all of his insides!

That serial had trapped him. And he fell for it. Dumb, dumb, dumb.

He had entered the warehouse without a gun. He never used a gun. Neighborhood talk led him to the abandoned warehouse on the suspicion a thirteen-year-old boy had been lured into the filthy structure by some off-the-wall, psycho druggie. Ken hadn't wanted the thirteen-year-old to get hurt. That's what he told himself as he stepped through the broken window into the darkened building.

Damn! An acrid puff of white ammonia something whirled around him. He gagged. Pigeon shit! He had stepped in a years-high pile of pigeon shit!

His eyes watered. The gritting white puff was on his face. He blew his nose. Damn stuff had flown up into his nostrils. Where were nose hairs when you needed them? Well, if stealth was his objective, the pigeon shit had become an alarm. He was in the building, and anyone waiting for him now knew it too.

He started to search for the thirteen-year-old. He let

his eyes adjust to the dank darkness inside the ware-house. He started to move, careful to avoid any more soft spongy piles!

Young boys had been disappearing for several months, an average one every two weeks. Not to be found. Parents were panicking, demanding something be done. As per usual, Chief Hutchins had assigned O'Hara to the case no one else wanted or had even the vaguest notion where to begin.

"You sure your son didn't runaway?" Ken'd asked parent after parent.

"Not my son!" was the standard reply, with varia-tions of—"I treat my boy right", "No, he isn't into drugs. Not the hard stuff, anyway", "He didn't run off with no girl. He's too young to have sex. But if he wants, he knows he's welcome to bring her home. Not go running off somewhere to have his fun" and "Please, can you find him, my son? Please, please—"

After questioning the nine sets of parents and/or guardians, plus a computer check on the national run-away hotlines, Ken concluded—as had Chief Hutchins and two other detectives, Lott and Morrisey—the boys weren't runaways. Most probably, the boys were snatched as playthings for some wielded-out ped.

That conclusion after one was found. Parts of one were more factual, in a trash can near a hospital: a penis with bite marks, an ear cut in two, a foot with suck marks. Could've been anybody, true. But when you've got noth-ing to go on, and nine boys lost, missing, presumed dead, several mutilated body parts were a find.

For several hours, Ken had toyed with the idea of trying to look like a young kid himself. After all, didn't people tell him he could pass for ten years younger than his actual age? He loved that! Still being carded at 32!

But even if he could appear to be seventeen, the boys disappearing were much, much younger and slight of build. Ken didn't fit the description of those favored by the sicko apparently prowling the streets, ravenous for young kids' male flesh.

So when word came through a snitch that a thirteen-year-old had been seen entering the abandoned factory warehouse with someone unfamiliar in the neighborhood, O'Hara followed up. Not much of a lead, but something. But why he never suspected the snitch was a set-up was a good question.

At the far end of the warehouse, Ken could see— what? He approached slowly. Every several feet, he had to slide an empty box or a wooden skid out of his way with his foot. Oil and grease slicks underneath made him even more cautious than if it were the usual pigeon shit.

Twenty feet away, he could see a large flashlight's beam was trained on something hanging from the ceiling's metal girders. He moved closer. Whatever it was didn't move. Why the flashlight?

Ken looked around the darkened building. Not a sound. He looked back toward the object of the flashlight's focus.

Oh, shit! It was a bare ass. Blood running everywhere.

Habit or learned response, Ken's first instinct was to rescue the boy. He moved closer. *Oh, shit!* Saw he was too late. No movement of any kind was happening anywhere within the boy's body except for his legs swinging back and forth, slightly.

Ken moved closer, and as his eyes focused to the flashlight's dim light—*oh shit!* he saw the boy was suspended from the ceiling's metal girders by thin wires wrapped tightly around his wrists. Streaks of dried blood slid from the wrists, down the boy's thin bare arms, matting the short blonde hairs in his armpits, some shaved off, it looked to Ken. Claw marks ran down the dead boy's arms. His chest was turning blue and had been scraped by a sharp object. His genitals had been completely cut off.

Ken reached to cut the boy down.

Suddenly his back was stung! Sharp! A cracking leather whip snapped, cut, and whipped him backward.

The psycho was on him, around him, jabbing. Over him, threatening, wielding a bloody butcher knife about to be rammed down into his neck. In a second, Ken rolled. The sharp blade bit into his shoulder instead of his neck. Bit and was turned, fast. Then sawing. Sending jolts of mega-pain throughout Ken's body.

He rolled out from under the psycho, knocking the flashlight from its perch. The sudden hard impact ended the flashlight's life. The warehouse went completely black.

His assailant laughed with delight at the darkness. He loved the darkness. His whip lashed through the air, snapping, lashing, twisting around Ken's neck, bringing the psycho jollies. The ped jerked the whip backward, quick, fast! More fun for him! Oh, boy! The whip tightened around Ken's neck. His hands flew up to pull off the whip.

Another backward jerk and Ken was on the floor. A rush slithered up and down the ped's body. What fun! He knifed Ken's shoulder again! More fun! The assailant stood up and jammed his boot into Ken's groin. Most fun!

Ken went unconscious.

An hour later, when he was dimly aware, he found

himself stripped naked and hanging from the ceiling's metal girders.

"Not again!" he gasped, stepping into the shower, hoping, dear God, the jets of hot water would wash away the memory, knowing they wouldn't.

Chapter 6

Later that evening, a few blocks south of New York University, in the middle of the Village, on the third floor of an ancient brick building probably built in the 30's, painted and gaudily muralled by the WPA, Master Wayne Welling sat on the hardwood training floor. Meditating in his dojo, which was also part of his home.

Every inch of the room bespoke a half-century-plus of martial arts excellence. Indeed, the dojo was a reflection of this master instructor. Trophies from worldwide tournaments filled several cases. Pictures of grinning, happy, competition-winning students, all belt and degree levels, covered three walls. Calligraphy and martial arts weapons covered the fourth.

Master Welling, a gracious kindly spirit encased within a well- disciplined, rock-hard body, heard the snap. Off in the distance.

A floor beneath him. Now—*snap*—on the stairs leading upward, to his floor.

The faint sound came closer, entering the room where he had trained some of the world's best fighters.

Now walking onto the training floor. With quiet firmness, he noted, "Your spirit is unclean."

Having given his assessment, Master Welling did not move. Instead he continued to focus himself, though he sensed constant movement all around. Had he looked he would have seen a high-tech compact video camera and a cellular phone being placed in a position quite close to himself. Had he turned he would have seen he was looking into the lens of the camera. But he didn't turn, he didn't look, quietly saying instead, "No shoes allowed on the dojo floor" to what sounded much like heavy boots.

Hearing, but not respecting the master's wishes, the intruder grabbed a bamboo fighting stick from along the wall and shouting, "Hajime!" jumped and leaped toward the meditating master. Slicing and thwacking the air around the elderly instructor.

Thwap! The stick cut the air and slammed to the floor an inch from master Welling's bent right knee, not moving, continuing in meditation position.

Thwap! An inch away from the bent left knee.

Thwap! An inch over the master's bowed head.

From her position in the precinct's central command center, Lt. Donna Collins was routinely monitoring several computer screens simultaneously. One screen, state-of-the-art and directly linked to a satellite, indicated the location of most of the Village precinct's seventy-five patrolmen as they moved about their respective beats, either on foot or in their cars.

Suddenly, for a quick moment, the satellite screen went black. A second later, it flashed a picture of a long-haired, sleek-bodied younger man slashing the air with a bamboo stick, an older fighter whipping his right leg high into the air, sidekicking and smashing the fighting stick out of the younger's hand.

The younger, bare-chested and wearing black gi pants, reacted violently. He spun around, leaping high into the air circling the other.

Landing near where the stick had bounced to the floor, the younger grabbed the stick and, with all his force, swung the stick horizontally. The stick slammed into the older man's back, just above his kidneys. The older man didn't appear to react, as if not even hit. The older's non-reaction angered the younger, who spun and swung the stick, aiming again for the master's muscled mid-back and kidneys. Blocked by the master's stick, the younger's stick whizzed toward the master's shoulders and was thrown upward with such a focused force that it sent the younger flying backward. He lost his footing and was thrilled by the challenge. Enervated. Back up! Adrenaline pumping. Hyped! Stronger than ever! About to explode!

"What's this?" Lt. Collins howled. "A kung fu movie on satellite?"

Several other officers on duty in the command center rushed to gather around the monitor. "Who's feeding us this entertainment?" one of them asked Collins who was wowed by the younger fighter.

He was hot, a body-builder. She'd sign up as a member of his fan club in a heartbeat.

The younger exploded! Out of control!

The older focused: quiet, patient, waiting.

The younger shot out a powerful low kick. He spun and swept his leg around, fast, cutting down the older at the knees. The older slipped slightly, almost unnoticed. But enough!

Seizing this slight opportunity, the younger slammed into the older time after time, now making hard body contact with his fighting stick.

THWAP! THWAP! THWAP!

"What goes here?" Officer Hendon asked Lt. Collins. He spoke louder so the lieutenant'd take her gazing eyes off the young fighter and bring herself back to the job. "What goes here?" again, louder.

"Just started coming in," Donna said, flustered. "I don't know who's sending it, but it looks like a Hong Kong action movie to me."

"Quality really sucks," Hendon observed to a chorus of "Yeah, man!" from the gawking group of command center officers as the younger whirled around, snapping his foot, striking the older fighter's helmeted head, momentarily stunning him.

The younger whirled toward the wall, leaped high into the air, spun around and whirled toward the older, spinning, chopping down into the older's breastplate, slicing it in two. The breastplate split, fell to the training floor as the younger whirled back toward the wall, grabbing and pulling off the wall a razor sharp live blade.

"Where's this coming from?" Hendon asked Collins, who was now trying to determine the point of origin of the show.

"Where's what coming from?" Burke asked, entering the command center. He moved closer to Lt. Collins. A flick of his wrist and he magically pulled a piece of candy out of her ear! He handed the red crystal chunk to her.

"This!" Hendon pointed toward the computer screen just as the younger, booted fighter twirled, swung and slammed the sharp blade into the older's now exposed chest. Blood burst toward the screen.

"What the hell?" Burke said, backing off as if splattered by the flying blood.

"I don't know what this is." Lt. Collins' fingers were rapidly moving over the keyboard, hitting one command, then another, clicking once, twice, sending "search" messages, trying to get a read on what was coming over the screen, getting nothing. "I can't trace it from here."

The younger fighter rammed the blade against the older fighter's helmet. With a deft, practiced skill, the younger pressed and twisted, slicing off Master Welling's helmet. Like the breastplate, the split helmet fell to the training floor, revealing the old fighter's wizened face. The younger, loving it, pressed the blade against the master's exposed temple, thrilled. The feel of an impending killing exciting him. Please, more challenge! More challenge! Don't let your death come too soon. He was hardening.

Master Welling, the coach who had taught so many, "Only fighters that want to win on this floor!" was leaving the floor, mentally. He didn't move, barely breathed. He struggled to bring himself back. He focused on the younger taunting, delighted eyes as the sharp blade whizzed and slit the skin along his right temple. "Hate you, motherfucker!" the intruder sneered.

WHAM!

Master Welling's foot shot upward. Connecting!

The blade flew out of the younger's hand and sailed across the room, ricocheting off the wall, plopping to the floor.

"Son of a bitch!" the younger fighter screamed his contempt for the old master.

WHAM!

With everything left in him, the fading master flipped up, vengeance aggressively surging through him. All his life he had taught respect for life. Hurt only when about to be harmed. He was bleeding from the head, his chest sliced open, he was summoning up an inner strength that was beating back his fading out, turning him into a tiger ready to jump, springing toward his attacker kicking.

"Yes!" the younger shouted in his mind. He blocked Master Welling's kick. He dropped, rolled, and went for the blade. Got it. Turning, springing upward, slashing the air with the blade. Wanting to cut! Thrusting, jabbing. Wanting to drive the metal deep into the flesh!

Spinning toward Welling, turning, sidekicking.

Connecting!

Rolling backward. Springing up. Jump kicking a powerful roundhouse into Welling's ribs. The master split blood.

What a wonderful feeling! Watching the master's life force being forced out of the life.

His ribs! His lungs! His upper chest! All his insides screamed with pain. Yet still he focused. Forcing himself from fading, willing himself back. Observing his attacker's whirling spin. A second later, his attacker now very close, his foot high in the air, almost on top of him, Master Welling, choking on his own blood, threw the ball of his right foot upward. It slipped past his attacker's raised, ramming leg.

Welling quick snapped his foot into his attacker's face. Connecting!

The younger spit blood, gasped for air. But thrilled! What a show he must be giving that Burke!

He rotated, rage propelling him, again out of control, slamming his foot into the master's stomach, into the master's head, into the master's groin.

Welling went down.

"Oh my God! I know him!" Chuck yelled. "That's no action movie! Get units to 562 Bleeker right away!" he shouted as he ran out of the command center. "And copy that transmission."

In the dojo, the booted fighter scrambled once again for the blade; Welling crawled across the floor for his fighting stick.

The intruder swung the blade. He wanted to feel the thwack, hear the thud of a decapitation. What the hell! Keep entertaining the cops who must be watching, must be wondering just a bit longer! Give 'em more time to make the connection—and to get here. He swung the blade at the older's raised bamboo stick. Snarling as he did so, really, really wanting to end this master's life, the life that had shamed him, that had made him feel a loser a year ago, the intruder sliced the bamboo shiniai to pieces. Then—what the hell!—he jammed the blade toward the master's neck.

The blade coming, unstoppable, the master asked, quietly, almost gently, "Who are you?"

The master didn't recognize him! *Didn't Recognize Him*! That fact might as well have been a bullet through the younger's heart, shot point blank.

"You don't remember me?" the intruder sneered. He then spewed out in insulted rage, "Pity!" He threw down the blade. Now more than ever, he wanted to feel this master's death in his own hands. He moved into a fighting position.

The master did likewise, watching the younger's tightening fists, tensing leg muscles.

The younger did a high kick to the master's chest. The master stepped backward, deflecting the kick. The younger spun again, hitting the master's neck with a quick snap, the ball of his foot ramming into Welling's windpipe. The wind flew of him. He flew against the wall. The younger threw a knife hand into his neck. Another. Another.

Pounding. Pounding.

Welling's windpipe crumbled under the pounding assault.

Then a back hand slammed into his. The master dropped.

Another quick snap as the master was sliding to the floor.

"Who's the champion now?" the younger viciously yelled. His fist slammed into the master's deadening eye sockets. "Answer me!" he screamed. "Damn it, *Answer me! Who's the champion now?*" His black eyebrows flying upward, into his head of shiny black hair, roiling with sweat. "*Who's the champion now? Who's the champion now?*" he demanded from the limp mass. "*Who's the champion now?*" He kicked the master in the kidneys, again, again, his powerful instep a spitfire repeater, rapid blows shooting into a lifeless form.

Squad cars sirens screeched through the night, racing toward 562 Bleeker. Skidding to a loud stop seconds after Burke had jumped off his Triumph.

Pulling his gun, Burke motioned the other officers to take cover and to cover him as he moved cautiously toward the building's street-side door.

About to step inside—*Whoosh*, the building exploded, windows and doors shooting outward, bright orange flames thrust upward toward the night sky. Shattered glass, massive chunks of burning wood, brick and concrete slabs flying toward Burke.

Ken fumbled for the ringing phone on the night stand.

"Ken?" the voice sounded urgent.

"Yeah?" Ken recognized the voice. "Hutch."

"No!" Ken's said, reaching to put the phone back on the night table.

"Your instructor, Wayne Welling, has just been killed."

Chapter 7

5—4—3—and then she was "Live from the scene."

"Late last night the murderer we're told police are now calling "The killer" struck again. The killer savagely beat to death a kindly, aged martial arts instructor, then blew up the martial arts instructor's place of business. The martial arts instructor also lived in a section of the building. That part of the building was partially destroyed by the explosion.

"Police Chief Hutchins again today refused comment as to whether or not master martial arts instructor Wayne Welling, 64, was murdered by the same killer who has now added a seventh victim to his list of horrifyingly violent murders. Chief Hutchins also refused to link any of the seven recent savage murders to one individual. Chief Hutchins said he did not want to prejudice any future jury members with any theories or pretrial publicity at this time. He has maintained such a reason for his total silence and non-co-operation with the press throughout this whole terrifying ordeal.

"Sources inside the police department, however,

again confirmed—on the condition of not being named—Kenpo Master Welling, a teacher and mentor to many, many Lower East Side neighborhood and city boys, teenagers and martial artists, bore deep bruising marks and wounds very similar to those of the other seven murder victims. This killer uses excessive force, apparently ruthlessly.

"The source went on to say what the police might be dealing with is a sadistic killer skilled in the use of deadly force, though the source would not confirm this statement.

"One interesting note to this case: rumors are circulating throughout the police department a high-tech video of the killing in progress was fed via satellite into police command central, a rumor Chief Hutchins would neither deny or confirm.

"One can only wonder, 'Who will be next?' and 'Why aren't the police doing something?' Kim Hunter, WGSN News, live from the scene, with crime-cam."

Chapter 8

"Thanks for coming, Ken," Chief Hutchins seem genuinely appreciative. His hand was extended toward his former thorn-in-the-flesh. "Sorry for your loss."

"Thanks," Ken nodded. "He was a great man." Then, knowing he was back, Ken got right to business. "What do we have?"

Chief Hutchins pointed to Chuck, an indication of who was in charge.

"I'll let Detective. Burke bring you up to speed, okay? You are to work together, as partners, on this case."

Ken nodded toward, acknowledging Chuck's leadership. Burke shot out his hand, begrudgingly. They shook, Chuck saying, an edge to his tone, "Glad to have you on board, O'Hara." Since Chief Hutchins was standing right beside him, he forced himself to add, "We can sure use your help."

Chuck was careful not to tip his hand that, even though he was still in charge, he felt demoted. As if Chief Hutchins thought he couldn't handle this case. Holy fuckin' damn, he'd been working on this case, chasing down every lead, spending hundreds of hours day and night for three or four months now. Nothing else. He gestured down the hall to Ken.

"Why don't you come into my office?"

"Lead the way." Ken was eager to get started.

"Later," Chief Hutchins said as the two men moved toward Detective. Burke's office. "Thanks again for helping us out, O'Hara." His words burned Chuck's tail.

"You read the file?" Chuck asked as the two walked side-by-side toward his office.

"Carefully."

"And?"

"Department's not getting anywhere, huh?"

Wham! A verbal chop to Chuck's investigative short hairs.

"That's why you're here, O'Hara." Chuck fought to seem cordial, even complimentary, as the two entered his office. "You got any ideas?"

"We're dealing with a very organized killer," Ken started in right away. "This killer plans. His killings aren't random, spur of the moment things." Without being asked, he seated himself across from Chuck's desk. He stared at the taunting messages hung up on Chuck's bulletin board, continuing his draw on the killer. "He only kills who he wants to kill. Low risk victims in low risk areas, no witnesses." Ken paused to eye Burke. Was he telling this guy new poop? O'Hara saw disdain for him in Detective. Burke's eyes rather than interest in his theories. Burke was champing at the bit. Nevertheless, Ken barreled on. "Everything's planned out very well. The killer's behavior reflects his personality, and his behavior is very controlled, well-orchestrated. His M.O. exists nowhere else. Now, I thought—"

"Let me stop you right there." Chuck was firm. "I

know who you are, O'Hara. You quit the force because you were scared. I can't partner with a guy who is going to piss himself whenever he comes face-to-face with the enemy. So you can have all the bullshit theories you want and write all the stupid reports, but stay the fuck out of my way when it gets dirty. You got that?"

Ken stared him down, just as firm.

"Yeah. I got that."

"I'm sure Chief found you your own office. So why don't you find it?" Ken was getting dismissed. "I need to check out a theory." Chuck reached for his phone. "I'll call you."

As Ken stood to leave to find his own office, he gave an order of his own.

"I need copies of everything you got on the case," he was just as strong, just as firm as Burke had been, no-nonsense, now imitating Burke in word, gesture and tone, "for my stupid reports."

Chuck wasn't amused. Coldly, he replied, "My secretary'll get what you need."

Ken walked out Chuck's office door.

"And O'Hara," Chuck's words, a lighter tone in his voice, stopped Ken's exit. The two had dueled. O'Hara had sparred but hadn't injured his new partner. "Glad to have you onboard...Ken."

Ken nodded. "Thanks...Chuck."

✎

"No, dammit, I won't grant an interview to Kim Hunter!" Hutchins was firm. "Tell WGSN if they get in the way of this investigation in any way, I'll get a court order to gag them."

What was said on the other end of the line wasn't

heard because Hutchins slammed the phone down. He missed the phone's cradle and slapped the stack of paperwork instead. Pissing him off more. "Damn!"

If O'Hara and Burke didn't turn up some leads soon, he'd...he'd screw 'em both professionally. Oh, hell, he wouldn't do that; that'd make him look like a real asshole. He didn't know what he'd do! Maybe he'd go back to teaching in the police academy where he didn't constantly have someone looking over his shoulder every minute questioning his every attempt to get something done. And, hell, this wasn't the only weirdo murderer the city had running loose right now. Investigators were sent to five other murder scenes this morning. True, half of those murders were spousal-caused. Why didn't WGSN go after those, do "live from the scene" as some beer-swilling hairy back slugged his wife, then did her in? *Focus your cameras where society could be changed*, he thought, *not on some sicko psycho who was a psychological aberration, not come after the chief of police who had absolutely nothing to do with this weirdo and couldn't just suddenly pull a rabbit out of the hat to end this serial's killing. Oh, hell, don't say that; Burke could! Pull a rabbit out of the hat, that is. Apparently, not solve this case, however!*

Hutchins picked up the morning paper and walked down the hall toward the men's room. Mumbling, "Let 'em try to find me there."

Detective. Burke pulled open the forty-year-old file cabinet, thumbed through a hundred "open" file folders, finally finding and pulling out the folder containing pictures of the destruction of Master Welling and his dojo. He sat down and scanned every corner of each picture.

What could he learn from these pictures? Who was

this savage killer? Why Master Welling? What was the killer's connection to the master instructor? A student, perhaps? Why ice so kindly a man who'd been honored by the city for building character in youth? And do so so savagely to boot. What moved this killer? How was he selecting his victims? And who'd be next? *Damn, something's got to be here!* Chuck thought, even though he probably had to admit O'Hara was right. This killer was so ballsy he'd sent taunting messages to the police, so arrogant he'd thumb his nose at the police by feeding video of the murder the very moment he was killing the master to the police. This kind of killer didn't make mistakes. Not the kind that would immediately trigger investigative responses from the police.

But he had to try to find something. His job and well-being depended on it.

Burke squinted at the pictures. Yet what he saw was what he expected to see. Charred remains, blackened walls, glass blown out of window frames, a door frame without a door. But something didn't seem quite right. What? What? *Damn! what?*

He scrutinized the gruesome pictures, every angle, every inch, urging himself to see what wasn't there.

Finally, his eyes tired but his mind telling him he had to, he buzzed his secretary.

"Margie, I'm outta here for an hour."

"Yes, Detective. Burke," Margie answered back, knowing full well her boss almost always got so involved whenever he left the office to work on a case, he'd probably not be back for the remainder of the day. What'd she tell the chief to that? Maybe she'd make her herself a hair appointment.

Burke closed the folder and returned it to the file cabinet, putting the picture-crammed folder at the front of the cabinet's top drawer this time. Then he walked out the door of his office and down the hall into the elevator. The elevator doors opened. He pushed G. The doors closed. Two floors down, he stepped out of the elevator, strode out the front door and climbed onto his cycle.

Fifteen minutes later, he was lifting up, stooping under the yellow crime scene tape warning all the squatty brick building was "Off limits." He stepped over a pile of debris blown onto the sidewalk last night. He entered the building, careful where he placed his feet. The smell of burned, charred wood immediately smacked him in the face.

He climbed the staircase to the third floor: Master Welling's dojo and home.

The dojo was dark. The smell of charred, burned wood was much more pungent here than below on either the second or ground floors. He felt his way along the wall.

He suddenly stopped.

He sensed someone else was in the dojo. From the sound of it, feeling his way along the far wall.

Chuck froze.

Whoever it was stepped away from the far wall. Stopped. Froze. Apparently listening, probably trying to figure out who else was in the blown-out dojo.

Chuck waited. The only noise now heard in the room the *zzzing-zzzing* buzzing of a cracking neon sign flickering on and off, bright then low, across the street. Occasionally, the sign flashed bright enough for a quick second, very faintly red-lighting the dojo. But only enough to show the outline of another individual frozen in wait.

Chuck took a step toward the outlined individual. Still in total blackness. His cautious step was suddenly countered by a snap kick to his chest. Chuck was slammed backward, knocked off his feet. He sprung upward, pounding his attacker with clenched fists made hard through years of training and on-the-job use.

His attacker fought back, ramming a fist into Chuck's stomach. Chuck reached out to grab his attacker, who leaped backward, spun around and did a fast low kick into Chuck's knees. The police detective went down.

Suddenly, as if just refilled with gas, the neon flashed bright again just as the attacker was about to pound Chuck's face with his fist.

Another neon flash. Chuck recognized the attacker. "You! What're you doing here?"

Chuck's snapped snarl stopped the fist in mid-strike. "My job. Remember?"

"Man, you're lucky I didn't kill you." Chuck shoved O'Hara off him.

"Yeah, I'm positively blessed." Ken didn't waste effort disguising his sarcasm.

"Thought I told you to stay out of my way." Chuck pounded Ken verbally. "You come over here to sneak around in the dark?"

"I'm picking up impressions." Ken corrected his partner/boss.

"Well, pick up your butt on your way out," Chuck chided the detective who prided himself on unorthodox, sometimes legally questionable methods, "because I'm about to kick it."

"My knees are shaking," Ken's tone teased Chuck, who took Ken's teasing as a slam. He poked Ken. Who jabbed back.

A flashlight beam suddenly caught both men in mid-clash.

"What the hell's going on here?"

Chuck's hand whipped into his shirt pocket, a flick of his wrist, a sleight of hand. He flashed his badge.

"Police officer. Who are you?"

"I live here," came the reply.

"The victim lived here alone." Chuck corrected the stranger standing in the darkness.

"Kelly?" Ken asked. "That you?"

"Uncle Ken?" the female voice asked, rushing toward O'Hara, falling into his out-stretched arms, and sobbed, "My father—"

"Uncle Ken?" Chuck, his eyebrows flying upward in disbelief, turned toward Ken, suspicious.

"It's okay," Ken assured Chuck. "This is Master Welling's daughter, Kelly."

Chuck backed off a few minutes as Ken comforted the sobbing Kelly. Then, "I feel for your loss, Miss, but I'd like to ask you some questions. How about we go down to the station?"

Kelly grimaced, shaking her head.

"We can talk tomorrow, Kelly," Ken countered Chuck's request. "Don't worry."

Realizing he was a bit too quick in his demand, again backing off and trying to make up it some way, Chuck added, "The department will put you up in a hotel."

Not interested in a hotel the police might provide, but moreso in what really mattered, Kelly asked, "You got any leads?"

"That's what we're doing here," Chuck answered. "Working on them."

"Looked like you were working on each other." She was blunt, honest.

"Yeah, well...." Ken couldn't quite come up with an explanation to explain away the two detective's constant snipping at one another, so he offered, aping Chuck, "Let me take you to a hotel."

"That's okay. I'm staying with a friend. She's got an apartment near here. It was great to see you, Uncle Ken. I'll see you tomorrow."

"You bet," he said as Kelly made her way out of the dojo, part of which had also doubled as her home with her father until some sicko invaded and trashed her home and life. Forever.

When she was gone: "We should have questioned her tonight, 'Uncle Ken'." Chuck sounded pissed. "Don't go making decisions you don't have the authority to make." He was.

"Tomorrow's soon enough to talk with her." Ken walked away from his snipping partner. He bent down near the blown-out window, knelt on the floor, moved his open palms slowly across the hardwood surface, swishing away some bits of charred wood, glass. The flashing neon cast an eerie glow on the floor.

"When I'm the retired chicken shit," Chuck carped, "and you're running the investigation, you get to make the calls. But for now, asshole, stay out of my way!"

Ken didn't respond. Instead he kept swishing, searching.

"I'm calling it a night." Chuck began making his way out of the room. "You can skulk around here all you want in the dark."

Ken stood up. "I'm through skulking." He made his way toward the door, adding, just for Chuck, "For now."

The partners walked down the stairs, out the building together, Burke to his Triumph, O'Hara to his Honda, both totally unaware they were being watched.

Chapter 9

Next morning at the station at seven, Chief Hutchins looked at his two wonder boys, urgency written all over his face. Two more reporters had phoned his home before six, fishing. "What's the latest?" "What's being done?" "Any suspects?" His non-answer grunts turned their questions into accusations. "Department's caving in on this one, huh?" "Whole city's forced to look over their shoulders all day because of some psycho serial, but not to worry, we're still out there writing our quota of parking and jay-walking tickets! That it, Chief?"

So Hutchins had to beat up on his two detectives, demanding the impossible: "You guys find something about this psycho! And you better fucking find it today!"

Ken felt his chief's pressured frustration. He wanted to tell Hutch what all three of them already knew. What each had experienced for the last ten years. Detective work's become a very slow, methodical, better-be-right process. Rush something through, without being open-and-shut two hundred percent certain, sure as anything, and some cocksure lawyer'll fry your balls in court, make you look like creamed shit while the perp ends up appearing to be little Red Riding Hood about to be savaged by the big bad wolf: the cops. And in the end, the lawyers'll do it every time: the perp walks. Rush this one like others in the past, justice will not be served; the city will have expended a pile of taxpayers' money only to have its police force made to look like incompetent fools who can't even wipe their asses.

And never mind if you got shot or injured in the line of duty. Only thing the media and the public really understood was a cop's getting killed on the job. Then there was an outcry. But anything else was "Hey, I've got tough times on my job, too, pal. Work with it." Maybe Megan was right after all. This job was a thankless crock.

"There was no sign of forced entry," Ken began explaining to Hutch and Chuck, "and the explosive was pretty primitive—gasoline and a stick of dynamite. I didn't see a timer anywhere in the dojo. That means the killer had to have been waiting for Detective . Burke."

Chuck appeared bewildered.

"How do you know that?"

"Skulking," Ken winked at his partner who felt one-upped. The retired detective—now back—continued: "Killer must have been waiting for Burke to come running into the dojo. Maybe he's tied into our GPS system so he can track our vehicles. Anyway, he blew the place up a second before Burke went inside."

"He was out to get Burke?" Hutch asked.

Ken shook his head.

"If Chuck's what he wanted, he would have waited 'til Chuck was inside the building."

"Explosion covered his tracks?" the chief theorized.

"More like the killer's playing with us." Mindhunter Ken sounded like he already had a handle on this psycho. "He wants us to see his work. As if he's tantalizing us, daring us to catch him in action. Why else the video feed into our system?"

Against his better judgment and three months of work on this case, Chuck had to admit inside himself where Ken was going with this sounded right. Or at least, more than he had. Shit, not even back a day and already taking over.

"The killer's sending us a message," Ken sounded more and more certain. "His killings are getting closer together, and he's getting better. It's almost as if he's learning. He's getting more confident, so he's sending us the computer notes, taunting us. This guy is so out there with technology, and I'm," Ken threw up his hands, "lost."

Ditto Hutch and, though he wouldn't admit it, not to O'Hara's face, ditto Chuck.

"I know a computer hacker from a case a couple years ago. I want to go see him, Chief, get some advice on the computer end of things."

Hutch looked at Chuck, who could only nod his agreement, as if "yeah, sure, I've worked my ass of on this case three months, you solve it in a day, arrogant bastard." So he had to say to O'Hara, "Well, don't stand around here then."

"We're gone," Chuck sounded determined, heading toward the door.

Outside the conference room, Chuck couldn't resist.

"You really burned my ass in there."

Ken didn't break stride, didn't bother to respond to such pettiness.

Inside he was boiling to himself, *Not enough to bust*

*your ass on some psycho serial, you gotta also look like
an ass to please your partner. Well, he wasn't on this
case to please no partner. He would fry that bastard
psycho murderer for what he'd done to his master
teacher. Then he'd go back into retirement. End of statement. No coming back. Ever! He'd find this fucking
weirdo, put 'im where he'd see less than ten minutes of
sun a day until he'd be burned sizzling black with a
mega-jolt he himself would volunteer to throw, then "that
was when the fat lady had sung!" He was outta here.
Back to getting a new life, a life that didn't include psychos, weirdos, sickos, or cops. Maybe Arnold needed
another scooper.*

The thought of Master Welling suddenly took him
back twenty-some years ago. He was 10, too tall standing beside others his age, much too skinny, all bones,
gangly, spindly, awkward always. Kids at school made
fun of him. Almost every day. "Mantis!" they called
him out on the playground because he held his long,
bony arms up, extended, letting his hands droop downward, indeed looking to many like the long, green, stick-
like praying mantis insect. Didn't help that his mother
said he'd grown out of this stage into a fine looking
man like his father. He needed to do something now. He
couldn't wait to grow out. His own self-awareness
needed something now. Then he'd shut up those name-
calling kids. But now?

Master Welling was there for him back then. An
instructor from the old school demanding total, complete, instant, unquestioning obedience to his every command, to his every whim, to his every directive, no matter how absurd. For weeks before he was accepted as a
beginner student, before he was even allowed to step on
the hardwood training floor of the master's dojo, gan-

gly Kenny was forced to prove his worthiness to be a student.

"You want to study martial arts?" Master Welling asked, slowly, patiently, with that far-away inscrutable look of wizened old masters.

"Yes, sir," he conveyed from deep-set, hoping, hollow eyes.

"Be here next Friday at six."

He was. He sat not on the training floor. "This floor's only for feet that want to learn how to kick!" Master Welling said with an authority that propelled 10-year-old spindly Kenny back up against the wall, saying, "I do, sir."

"Then sit there!" Master Welling pointed toward the far corner of the room, where a determined Kenny sat for three hours, not moving, stoically watching the others train, learning techniques. He didn't complain, didn't say a word.

At 9:30 p.m., the class was over. Again, Master Welling asked the gangly, silent kid, "You want to study martial arts?"

"Yes, sir," from impressed and desperately-longing eyes.

"Be here next Tuesday at six."

He was. Sitting again in the far corner of the room, after being told when he entered the dojo, "This floor's only for hands that want to block and chop." After answering honestly, "I do, sir." After being ordered, "Then sit there!" After being pointed toward the corner, where he again sat for three hours, not moving, eagerly watching the others block and chop, never once complaining, not for a second seeming to be tired or bored watching blocking and chopping.

At 9:30 p.m., the class over, again from a stern Master Welling, "You still want to study martial arts, kid?"

"I do, sir." More determined tonight than last Friday.

"Be here Friday at six."

He was. Not even going near the training floor. "This floor's only for those who want to be champions."

"I do, sir!" certain.

Master Welling looked the kid over. Scrutinized, actually. Could he take the rigid, unbending discipline expected? Could he check his ego at the training hall door and let himself be verbally bludgeoned into action or inaction three hours a night, three nights a week? Could he concentrate, focus, center himself on developing himself physically and inwardly? Would this little kid let others assist in building character, instilling integrity, developing loyalty, demanding discipline? Or would this gangly runt quit? Like so many other kids who shout, "I do, sir!" and then they don't.

"Nothing will make me quit, sir!" Kenny, his jaw set, his feet planted firmly on the floor, his eyes looking straight ahead, shouted out.

"Nothing?" the master snapped.

"Nothing, sir!"

And for the next three weeks in a row, every night of the three nights a week he showed up—trying his hardest to prove he wanted to begin martial arts training with Master Welling—he was ordered to "crawl on his hands and knees into the men's room," where he was to "stay on your hands and knees and scrub the urinal spit-shine clean" with the toothbrush being handed to him by an intimidating black belt third-degree student of the master.

And for the next three weeks in a row, every night of the three nights a week he showed up—just to try to begin martial arts training with Master Welling—he crawled into the men's room, stayed on his hands and knees and scrubbed the urinal with a toothbrush. Without questioning. Without complaining. Not a murmur. Without even a look or a thought or an uttered word that would indicate anything other than an unwavering desire deep down inside himself—growing more definite each night he was there—to study martial arts. He had a reason. A reason more important than any humiliation they could inflict upon him.

Not a word of complaint, not a murmur, not even when several black belts in their mid-twenties walked into the men's room—if the truth be known, sent in by their master. They stood smack up against the urinal, loosened the drawstrings around their gi pants, and pissed into the urinal, straight forward, as hard, as fast as they could push it out, splashing wetness and urine over toothbrush-wielding Kenny.

Still, from him, not a word.

Nine nights he hoped to be taught a kick, a move, a technique. Nine nights he hoped in vain. Nine nights he languished beside a urinal, scrubbing, wanting to learn, scrubbing, ignored. Now even by the urinal users. Nine nights he scrunched down—unseen—tight against the floor, near the bathroom door, straining, squinting to look through the tiny crack between the door's edge and the floor to catch a glimpse of Master Welling's instructing roundhouse kicks, leaps, spins, sidekicks.

On the tenth night, he was given permission to attend class and to walk on the training floor.

From the memory of what he had seen through the tiny slit, 10-year-old Kenny leaped and spun and kicked a roundhouse that so impressed Master Welling that the master teacher focused his attention on determining how this spindly kid did such a technique. Walking into the men's room a day later, scrutinizing the entire room, then—seeing the crack under the door—laying down on the floor to see if...?

So! He'd been out-foxed by this ten-year-old! He decided then and there to be even harder on this determined Kenny. He demanded more, always more, whenever he was training this kid.

So at 10, at 11, at 12, Kenny was forced to train barefoot and gi-clad outdoors in the middle of winter, standing in two feet of snow for as long as two hours, practicing kicks, one-steps, techniques and forms over and over again. Then, over and over again. Then again. And through all the repetition, never daring to let up under the ever-watchful eye of the master, Kenny battled to stay focused against the cold. Then center punch after center punch, his feet tingling, prickling from the snow's freezing wetness. Over and over again, center punch, center punch, center punch. The sleet-filled icy wind stinging his face, biting his neck, often turning his neck and face fiery red during the first half-hour of training, two hours later, a scary blue.

And always, from the master: "Gimme more kicks." "Gimme more one steps." "Those techniques are wrong. Focus! *Focus!*" "Concentrate!" Over and over again. Repetition upon repetition. Three hours a night, three nights a week, inside, outside, no matter the weather, no matter the temperature, practicing, being taught, being disciplined, always more, more, more, and when his energy ebbed, still more: running the fitness trail in the dead of freezing, sleeting winter; working out in unheated gyms or the nature park, constantly being urged to discipline his mind to "Forget! Forget!" all conditions around him: *"Focus, Focus"* only on what was happening inside himself; expected to do a thousand push-ups and a thousand sit-ups each week on his own and turn in a written statement attesting to his having done more than what was expected the first class of every week. No written statement that first class, no instruction for the next week; pushed through the nature park's ropes course, fifty feet up, zigging and zagging high above the ground between trees, once a week, without fail, regardless of wind, hail, sleet or snow. Not even the hot, blazing sun could keep "Hey, you, kid!" from being ordered up! Thunder, however, made Master Welling think a moment before pointing Kenny upward. The first streak of lightning got "Hey, you, kid!" pointed down.

And throughout this grueling, teaching treatment from Master Welling, Kenny's "example person," just one word of complaint, just one sign of hesitation, just one second's pulling back immediately from Kenny ended his training session! For the week! With the barked words, "Martial arts training is not for the weak, not for the timid!" hurled at him as if he was being weak, timid. When he was only tiring. Or needed a quick rest.

No matter!

"If you're not serious, if you don't want to work, keep your heiney home! I'm not wasting my time with no weak, timid kid!"

"I'm not, sir!"

"Prove it!"

Instantaneously spurring Kenny to work more, harder, with even more determination. Out of respect for his master instructor. Working and reciting the fighter's code: "Loyalty to country. Obedience to parents. Honor friendship. No retreat in battle. In fighting, choose with sense and honor," making determination, work, the code part of him.

Though strict and demanding, Master Wayne Welling had a heart, a personal warmth, an encouraging spirit, a quiet strengthening, some kind of enabling graciousness that wouldn't put anybody through what he himself hadn't been put through, made to endure. And out of this strict training and demanding, almost without Ken's own noticing, came self-respect, a developed self-confidence, a sense of physical and mental betterment.

He had grown into a man.

Master Welling had done that. No, he—Kenny—had done that. But with a major assist from his master. And now that strong, determined, encouraging master was dead. Viciously savaged by some weirdo psycho. And for what reason?

"Hi, Uncle Ken. I've been waiting all morning to see you." Ken swung around, the kindly-sounding voice pulling him out of his momentary reverie. Kelly was sitting on a long bench just outside the station's conference room. He must have walked right past her while he was inwardly fuming at his new partner and remembering his master, her father.

"What're you doing here?" was Ken's first response. He was caught off-guard by her voice and presence.

"I was told to be down here this morning, remember? The interview."

"Oh, yeah," he remembered. But something about Kelly's determined look told him she was here for more than a session of questioning.

"Sure," Detective. Burke jumped in quickly, "let's get to it. This way." He ambled toward an interview room just down the hall, not aware she wasn't following. Until—

She said, determination not to budge from her statement in her tone, "I want to be involved."

Her strong, firm words stopped both Ken and Chuck's entrance into the interview room. Ken turned, saw the determined Kelly still standing beside the bench. "You have to stay out of this," he said just as strongly, just as firmly. Yet knowing his words—no matter how strong—probably would do no good.

"What are you talking about?" Ken knew the fight was coming! "This was my dad!"

"Sorry, Kelly." He fought back, kindly. "Go home." He moved toward the young woman the master had made his god-daughter upon her birth, a title he took very seriously. He was there at her birthday parties. He went to her track meets. A couple times he spotted for her in the gym. He'd even been her sparring partner in the master's dojo when she was six and he was twenty. Even back then, she'd knocked him on his butt more than once. But look who's daughter she was. She'd been born kicking!

Just as she was doing now.

"Uncle Ken, please—!"

"Kelly, I'll call you when I know something."

"I want to help."

"No!"

"You think I can't?" Another verbal kick to his conscience!

"I know you could." He blocked.

"Then why?" A chop.

"I'm not the boss on this case." He deflected to Burke. He was retreating. Breaking the fighter's code!

"Yeah, right," she chopped them both down.

"Look, you're too attached." He came back. "Your feelings'll get in the way of doing the job."

A knee jerk.

"And yours won't?"

Stunned! Ken shrugged.

"It's not my decision, Kelly. I'm in retirement. Just pulled out on this one because this killer's got to be stopped."

"In other words, you wouldn't be here if it weren't my father?" Ken could feel the noose about to be pulled tighter. "Same with me."

"It's not my decision." Lame.

"I'm going to the chief!" And with that, she turned and headed toward Hutchins' office, a perfect opportunity for Ken and Chuck to turn and head toward their squad car, which they did.

Chapter 10

"This hacker friend of yours—"

"He's not a friend."

"Thought you said he was—"

"I said I used him on a case years ago."

Ken and Chuck were on each other—again—as Chuck drove to the general location Ken hoped to find the hacker.

"He lives just around that corner." Chuck turned the wheel in the direction Ken pointed. "Five years ago he did."

"Look, O'Hara," Burke continued harping, "you tag along with me," he turned the wheel, "you play by my rules."

Ken stared out his open window and remained silent. A tactic that irritated Chuck all the more.

"So, you and Kelly have a thing going."

Another zing to the detective's soft spot!

"She's like my daughter." Ken said. Then, realizing, "Oh, I get it. I don't think you're her type."

Stinging Chuck.

"Oh, really! Why? Because I'm black?"

"Because you're an asshole!" Ken shot back.

"Well, at least you're not a racist," Chuck retorted. He brought the car to a stop. "This hacker guy dangerous?"

"Only if you're allergic to poor hygiene," Ken said as he pushed open the squad car's door.

"You follow my lead," Chuck ordered, stepping in front of Ken. Ken side-stepped Chuck.

"I'll watch the back door, just in case."

⌁

He couldn't believe his eyes. She was gorgeous. Absolutely eye-popping, bulge-making gorgeous! And what she was asking him! He was fire all over. Wow! Wow! *Wow*! As she cooed, wetting her lips with her tongue—lusciously—"Shall I take off," she was teasing him, "my top?"

"Yeah, yeah, yeah!" he said so fast he couldn't get his zipper open, wishing she could do that, please! Saying, "You should definitely take off your top!" Slavering, "I bet you're hot, hot, hot! Aren't you?"

Justice, all 309 pounds of him jammed into a swivel desk chair, hunkered over his keyboard, clicking on the dancing sexy girl's image on the screen. One of her fingers was impishly beckoning him to come closer, much, much closer to her assets. So he clicked. Twice. And she was gone! Wiped out in a second click's blip.

"Damn! Damn! *Damn*!" he cursed. "Come back here, baby! Please!"

Suddenly, a knock at his door.

"Shit!" he spat, not turning toward the door, his fingers flying over the keyboard, trying to resurrect this

latest hot tamale. "What'd ya want?" to the computer ,
meant for the knocking door.

"Police!" Burke shouted from the third floor hallway. "Open up!"

Justice pushed "F5." The hot tamale re-appeared.
Sans panties, and she was wriggling back-and-forth.
Hotter than ever! He'd have to remember that command.
Her dainty fingers slipping upward and under the tiny,
tiny pencil thin straps that held her preciousness in place.
Both of them. He couldn't wait. He'd never seen this
babe before, at least not doing what she's suggesting
she's about to do, and if past programming held a key to
her endowments, she was one big handful! Ready to
put out! Justice could hardly contain himself. Where
was virtual reality when you needed it?

Burke knocked again.

"Open up! I need to ask you some questions."

"Why kind of questions?" Justice yelled, eyes glued
to pumping and grinding just beginning. He took his
fingers and hands off the keyboard. This was not the
time to hit any key or roll the mouse.

"Just open the door!" Chuck was getting impatient.

Justice was in a dilemma. He didn't want to lose
her. He didn't want to open the door. He didn't think
this insistent copper would just go away. He didn't want
her to go away. He couldn't stomach the police. He
wanted to watch her and dream.

Outside the door, Chuck pulled his gun.

"Listen in there. I'll blow the lock off if you don't
open up!"

"Hey, what ya doin' in this hallway?" an old hag,
her straggly hair standing straight up in a thousand directions, two decked out with purple ribbons, sniped.
She held a box of macaroni and cheese, the cheesier

kind, in her wrinkled, rutted hand and clunked the detective on the back. "No guns! No guns!" she jawed.

"Gotcha!" Justice was delighted. Ethel, the tenement snoop, had been true to her eldritch preoccupation: she watched everything, everybody, coming and going down the third floor hall and messed in their business. Once he had left the door open to his apartment a crack, quite by accident. She heard an "Ooh, just for you!" and, jar of stewed tomatoes in hand, popped in to have a look-see. When she saw him ogling the computer screen, his fingers like a giant chubby hairy spider's legs engulfing its prey, squeezing, squeezing, pinching, she thought she was living next to a perverted something or other and she'd be next! She opened the jar of stewed tomatoes—he was so into, "Ooh, just for you too, ooh!"—he never heard her struggling to twist the metal cap open. It wouldn't. Then, clunking it on a table's edge several times, trying to get the metal cap to move, twisting and twisting—finally—she emptied its contents all over him and her. Took him three days to get all the tomato parts off his keyboard. Three days without "Ooh, just for you!" and that made him ecstatic now that she was out there onto someone else. Maybe if he tinkered around here a bit longer in here, she'd dump her culinary specialties all over this irritating cop.

On the other hand, maybe the cop was in uniform and she had reported "Ooh, just for you!" as some violation of that damned new Internet law Clinton'd just signed. Damn him! "Ooh, just for you, too!" and he wasn't talking poozle!

Maybe it was time to—

Justice grabbed a duffel bag near the base of his work station, always packed, never used, for a one-night stand, and headed toward the open window. One step and he was out on the fire escape—greeted by, "Detective. O'Hara, Justice." Ken pushed the obese hacker back through the window. "Remember me?"

A grunt of recognition.

Ken saw the duffel bag in Justice's hand.

"You going somewhere?"

Another grunt.

Without taking an eye off Justice, Ken crossed to the door. He screwed with the deadbolt a second, then opened the door.

"You looking for him, Officer?" Just as dry macaroni was sprayed over Detective . Burke, wedding-style.

Pissed, Ken was already in the room, trying to be gentle and patient with the third floor loon, taking a step into the room, hearing a cracking, "Ooh, just for you, too, copper!" enduring another shower of dry macaroni, Burke turned and stared down the old crone. "Later, baby," he smiled and closed the door just as Ken shot out to the old hag, "He means it, too."

Chuck plowed into the room. He grabbed Justice by the throat.

"You messed with the wrong guy! You're coming with me!"

"For what?" Another grunt.

"Don't play dumb with me!" Chuck shouted. He threw Justice up against the wall. "We know all about you."

Ken just shook his head. Chuck was overplaying his hand.

But it worked.

"You mean the bank computer?" Justice sputtered. "I didn't do anything—"

"Of course you didn't!" Chuck was in Justice's face.

Ken sat down in the swivel desk chair. He admired

the last few seconds of the bawdy beauty before the screen-saver wiped her away with a gulping swallow by a giant fish-tailing barracuda. "Sorry, Justice. Detective . Burke and I don' t necessarily see eye-to-eye." Ken clicked the mouse, twice, thinking the beauty'd be vomited up, adding "Burke, I need his help,"—he was wrong; the gorged fish swam off—"with my investigation."

Burke jammed Justice's head back against the wall.

Ken tried another command.

The fish sank beneath the screen's edge.

"Open up! Open up!" shouted from the hallway. "Buncha perverts!"

"I'll help you! I'll help you!" Justice whined, his head clamped to the wall by Burke's tightening hand.

"Shut the hell up!" Burke yelled. "No way this scumbag is getting out of this!"

"C'mon, Chuck, he said he'd help." Ken rolled the mouse ball. Still no vixen. Disappointed, he turned to face Justice. "You'll help, right?"

"Yeah, yeah. Whatever you need."

Ken became all business.

"Can you trace e-mail, graphics files and other messages?"

"Sure. It's not hard."

"Buncha perverts! I'm calling the police!" Ethel meant it, too, as she sauntered back toward her apartment, really pissed she'd wasted a box of the cheesiest. She determined to call crime-stoppers. Maybe she'd get a reward for tipping off the police about these psychos down the hall from her. That'd make up for the macaroni. "Damned if it won't!" she mumbled shuffling back to her door, and if the reward was large enough, maybe even for that jar of stewed tomatoes she wasted on lard-ass.

Ken pulled two diskettes out of his pocket. He put them on Justice's keyboard.

"These were sent to the police station. Trace 'em for us."

Burke opened his hand.

Justice moved back to his swivel chair, which Ken vacated the second Justice left his whining position up against the wall.

The hacker slipped one of the diskettes into the floppy drive and clicked retrieve, pulling up the first file, which he scanned quickly. He was a man who knew what he was doing, what he was looking for.

"There's no return address. Can't do it. I have nothing to work from."

"What's this for?" Chuck held up a long-necked bottle he found beneath the bottom computer shelf.

"For my all-nighters." Justice answered, his eyes still glued to the screen. He tried various commands. "So I don't have to leave my computer."

"Coffee?" Chuck asked.

"Urine."

Chuck dropped the bottle to the floor, disgusted. He pulled his handkerchief out of his pocket and rubbed his hands clean. Several times.

"Man, you're disgusting."

An alarm bell went off on the computer. Justice brightened.

"Watch, I can trace this message. It's real time, coming in right now."

A click and he opened up the piece of incoming mail. A graphic filled the screen. A moon. A second later, blood spurted from the moon.

"What the hell?" Justice checked the message. "It's addressed to Ken O'Hara?"

"That's me." Ken was stunned.

"Then this Bud's for you." Justice moved out of the way slightly so Ken could have a better view of the incoming message.

"How'd anyone know you were here?" Chuck asked.

Justice slid his chair to a printer. He clicked on the printer and began printing out the incoming message. "Keep him talking," Justice urged Ken. "Type what you want to say, then hit 'return.' I can trace him from here."

Ken scanned the moon. The same graphic that had been sent to Burke at the station, just before the Cunningham incident. "Holy shit. It is him!"

"Talk to him now!" Justice yelled. "Lose the connection, I lose him."

Ken typed, "Who are you?"

The voice box in the computer squawked, "You don't know?"

"What the hell was that?" Ken wasn't expecting a voice reply to his written question.

"Speech synthesizer," Justice sounded condescending, in his mind thinking, "Virgins. Don't know their way around," and saying, "Keep talking."

Ken typed, "Can you prove who you say you are?"

"How's this?" the computer said, arrogantly.

The screen blipped. From the top down, etching in a graphic picture. A dead body. Blip. From the top down, another dead body. Blip. From the top down, another.

"Holy fucking shit!" Justice squirmed.

Ken typed, "I am Detective O'Hara."

"I know who you are. I know what you have been through, and where you'll be going."

Ken typed, "Where is that?"

"Straight to hell!" the computer boomed.

Ken wanted to smash his fist through the computer's squawk box.

"Almost got him!" Justice shouted. "Keep him talking."

Ken typed, "Why are you killing?"

"It's a game to see who will win—you two or me."

Chuck stuck his head closer to the screen.

"Huh?"

"Yes, I know Chuck Burke is with you," the computer barked.

Chuck backed away.

"Shit! This guy knows everything."

"Got the son of a bitch!" Justice chortled.

"Where?" Ken swung around to where Justice was busy hitting keys on another keyboard.

"Beijing. No wait, Tainan, Taiwan. No, that's just a blind. Anchorage, Los Angeles. This guy is good, really good."

"I will kill again, and you will—" the computer's voice taunted O'Hara and Burke.

"Moscow, Berlin," Justice said, admiration in his tone. "Even I couldn't do this."

"You gonna find him or what?" Ken demanded.

"Getting there, getting there," Justice said. "Miami, Harrisburg, hold on, hold on, bingo! Last location, 843 S. Main, #2A. That's—"

"Right around the corner!" Chuck yelled. "Let's go!"

Justice continued typing/talking as the cops flew out of the room.

Five minutes later they're in the apartment building at 843 S. Main. Both taking the steps four at a time.

Outside the door at #2A.

"Where's your gun?" as Chuck pulled his.

"Don't use one."

"Why the hell not?"

Ken deflected the question.

"You ready?"

"What's the plan?" Chuck asked.

"I kick the door down, you go in first, secure the room. I cover your ass."

"Some plan, white bwana without a gun! I better kick the door down."

"Why?"

"It's your idea, that's why. You white cops are always sending the brothers in first. I don't think so."

"Okay, let's do it together. One, two, three!"

Ken kicked the door in.

"Police! Freeze!" Chuck charged into the apartment, yelling, "Nobody move!" sweeping the apartment with his gun.

In the middle of the room, six drug dealers in mid-deal were taken by surprise. Burke trained his automatic on them. One of the dealers, apparently either not seeing Burke's gun aimed at the group of dealers or acting out of some sudden death wish, jumped up. In that same second, he pushed his stash behind his belt and down into his black bikini brief. He lurched toward Burke who reacted in a flash, shouting, "Unless you're growing, you better sit your ass down!"

The dazed dealer moved back and sat down.

"Now!" Burke shouted, "Where's the computer?"

Nobody answered.

"Where the fuck is it?" Chuck yelled. Nobody answered.

"Go check in the back!" Chuck yelled to Ken. "I got these guys."

"Who you talking to?" one of the dealers sneered.

"Shut the hell up!" Chuck snapped. "Take the back."

Chuck looked around the apartment, still keeping his gun pointed on the six.

"You're all alone, man," one of the six, a dangly ear-ringed dude, laughed.

Chuck took a quick glance back at the door. It was hanging open. Ken was nowhere to be seen.

"Where's your back-up, copper?" a writhing snake-tattooed snickered. The way he moved his arm made the snake look as if it were about to strike and bite.

"Shut up! If I want anything from you, I'll wake you up to ask you!" Chuck shouted.

"Your pal desert you, man?" Dangly took a step toward Burke, testing the man's metal.

"I've got two SWAT teams on their way here right now!" Chuck bluffed.

"I don't think so, dipshit." Dangly took another step toward Burke.

"How about one SWAT team and a K9 unit?" Was this copper trying to make a joke? Dangly pulled a blade. Zzp! It flicked open, toward Burke. "Say good-bye, asshole."

"Good-bye, asshole." Ken was behind the dealer. A roundhouse kick and the switchblade went sailing out of his hands.

Another high kick and the low life was thrown to the floor. The others jumped to surround O'Hara, who spun and slammed a side kick into two of them. They flew into the wall. A fourth rushed him. O'Hara slugged the fourth into the neck. His fierce thrust jabbing the wind out of him. The fourth reached for his neck and got caught by O'Hara's snapping foot. The fourth went down.

Burke's fist caught Dangly's advance. Dangly flew backward. Two others jumped toward Burke who slammed one in the face with a hard uppercut. He spun and kicked the other in the chest.

O'Hara hauled ass, whirling, spin-kicking, smashing his foot into three dealers stupid enough to have jumped back up and come after him. Burke grabbed the prick who'd jumped on his back. He rammed the dealer up against the wall and whipsawed his face back-and-forth the plastered wall, then flipped the bleeding bastard off his back, onto the floor. Out cold.

"What took you so long?" Chuck yelled, turning to help Ken.

"I was waiting for the right moment." A spin kick into the side of Dangly's head. If he could have, Ken would've snapped his foot downward, ripping Dangly's silvery balls right off his ear. Instead, his right foot shot upward and sent the balls smashing up against the wall, accompanied by the body wearing them.

"I could've been killed!" Burke protested.

"I wouldn't have waited *that* long!" Ken was honest.

Two more kicks from both, and the dealers were out of business. Closed for the day and quite a few days to come.

Chuck went to the phone, hung on the wall, and dialed, barking immediately upon being answered, "Yeah, pick-up at 843 S. Main, #2A." He turned to Ken.

"Thanks, man."

"Least I could do."

Chuck motioned to the back of the apartment.

"We gotta check for the computer."

"Not there," Ken assured his partner. "No computer."

"You took the time to look?" Chuck hung up the phone. "Let me get this straight. I'm in danger for my life, and you looked for the computer?"

"Yeah, I did. Get over it." Ken said.

A familiar voice suddenly taunted, "Cop assholes! Cop assholes! Cop assholes!"

Chuck, taking aim, made his way slowly, cautiously down the hallway.

"Cop assholes! Cop assholes!" getting louder.

Behind that door!

Chuck kicked open the closet door. Seeing a man with a gun pointed at him, he fired. His automatic blew a hole right through his own reflection. "Holy shit!"

"Nice shooting, Tex!" from the familiar voice, now beneath him.

Burke looked down. On the floor was a laptop, its screen open, a message waiting: You flatfoots are out of your league.

Give up or get dead! See you soon.

The message scrolls. A video clip of the Keystone Cops rolls onto the screen. A group of cops rushing into a bank after a gang of bank robbers! Clunking into each other in their frantic hurry to get through the door. As the frenzied cops clobbered each other, all of them falling to the ground, getting nowhere, the computer exploded.

Pissed, Chuck pushed "Off!" a second before three cruisers and a wagon arrived to do pick-up. Chuck grabbed the laptop, ordered the arriving officers to "Read 'em their rights, then book 'em!" and left the apartment building, making certain Ken by his side.

Chapter 11

"Shit!" Chuck looked again in the rearview mirror. "We got company."

"Huh!" Ken turned and looked back. "Lose 'em."

Not needing a second urging, Chuck stepped on the gas. The squad car sped forward. The car behind him also sped forward. At 45, Chuck rounded the corner into a one-way. The wrong way. He snapped on his siren and plowed his way through three cars careening to a halt. The car behind made the same maneuver.

A UPS truck turned into the one-way. Chuck swerved to the right, narrowly missing a bumper in his grill. The UPS truck slammed to a stop. The car behind easily swung out and around the cursing delivery man.

Chuck rounded the next corner, turned the wheel sharply and blocked the street sideways. The car behind's tires screaming in protest stopped. Inches from slamming into city property.

Ken jumped out of the cruiser and ran back to the car behind, yanking open the door, pulling out—

"Kelly!"

"Hi, Uncle Ken." Wriggling to get loose beneath the cop's tightening hand.

"Thought I told you to go home." The detective was stern. Shaking his finger at the wriggler.

"I have something to do." She was adamant.

Burke, now out of the squad car, was on top of Kelly.

"This is police business."

"Save it, Burke," spitfire reaction from the muscled beauty. "It's not illegal to follow you guys."

"Stay out of our way." Ken warned. He walked back to the squad car. Got in. So'd Burke.

"Damn insistent!" Burke muttered, starting the car, pulling it out of its blocking position.

"Always been that way." Ken added what Chuck already suspected.

"I don't need any more help." Chuck stated.

"Hear me pushing her?" Ken was defensive. Then he grinned, thinking of the slim beauty who, with a swift sidekick, could have knocked him on his can but instead just kept wriggling and wriggling. "Although she was a former national champion."

Miffed, Kelly watched Burke and O'Hara pull off. She got in her Accord and followed the two all day. She'd follow them all week, all month if she had to, until these two let her work on this case. After all, didn't Chief Hutchins say he welcomed "citizen involvement!"

She stepped on the gas, got her car moving and kept her eye on the unmarked cruiser ahead, unaware that five floors up the killer had his eye on her.

Chapter 12

"I want this bastard so bad!" Chuck threw the computer printer-outs down on his desk, disgusted. He'd spent all morning studying the print-outs and the e-mail messages hanging on his bulletin board. Everything mocked him every time he walked into his office. So, too, the department pics of Cunningham, Schultz, and Welling. He'd been comparing each photo, each message, all morning, searching again for something in these photos or messages that might trigger a thought, an association, an idea, anything.

"He's got to be leaving something behind," Ken stood in front of the bulletin board, reading and re-reading. "Everyone makes mistakes."

"Not this psycho," Chuck cursed under his breath. "Not yet."

"Check the print-out again," Ken suggested. "Maybe we missed something."

"For the hundredth time," Chuck was exasperated, "it's all standard stuff. you talking to him, him baiting you. He's got a wit, though."

"Don't give him too much credit, okay? Don't even give him a personality." Ken picked up several pages of the print-outs from Chuck's desk.

"Serial killers fit a profile—white, in their 30's and 40's, certain definable experiences: child abuse, deviant sexuality."

"Spare me the profiling lecture, okay?" Chuck snapped at Ken. He was now looking at the last page of the print-out from Justice's machine in his hands. "Hold on, I never saw this before."

"What?"

"The last line of his message. 'Say good-bye to Jim, Gene and the heroes. There's blood on the moon.' What the hell's that mean?"

"Got me. Outrageous ranting of a lunatic mind." For a moment, Ken was histrionic, not appreciated by his partner.

"Maybe they have something in common?" Chuck cut short Ken's dramatic performance. He started reeling off names: "Jim Nabors, Gene Hackman, Hogan's Heroes."

"Your mind works in weird ways, Chuck." Ken grinned, then started spieling off names himself, aping Chuck, actually. "Jim Carrey. Carrey Gene. Carrey's heroes?"

"He's going after someone named Carrey?" Chuck was trying to make something out of nothing.

"Shit, this is nuts. C'mon, let's get something to eat." Ken reached for the phone. "I'm gonna check on Kelly at her friend's place."

Chuck stared at the photos and the messages as Ken dialed.

"I can feel the son of a bitch laughing at us."

"Wait a minute—Kelly!" Ken was trying to do another word association, word-by-word. "Jim Kelly, the guy from 'Enter the Dragon,' Gene Kelly, Kelly's Heroes. That's it! He's going after Kelly. While we're here chasing a ghost—"

There was no answer on the other end of the phone.

She ran toward the ringing phone. She had just come in, having been out getting burger, when she heard the phone ringing as she unlocked the door to her friend's apartment.

She picked up and heard the dial tone answering back her "Hello."

"Oh, well," she shrugged. "They'll call again if it's important."

She glanced at the decorative wall clock across the living room. 9:30. She'd get a quick shower, perking herself up a bit, then quickly head out for the second day of tailing those two. Maybe today would be the day they'd get so irritated having her hang around, they'd have to let her help on this case.

Determined, she headed toward the bathroom. Inside the tiny room, she began undressing. She slipped out of her jeans, then pulled the sweatshirt up and off.

Snap.

Kelly unsnapped her bra and slid out of her panties. Took a quick glance at herself in the mirror. Still sleek. She pinched her side near her waist. Hardly could. Keep eating those veggies. Lay off those grand slams!

Snap.

Her senses alerted.

"Jill, you home? Thought you went to work? I'll be out in a minute."

No answer.

"Jill?"

No answer. All was quiet.

Passing it off, Kelly stepped into the shower. She pushed the big plastic knob up and slightly to the left. Instant swirling jet stream.

The noise of the spitting water jets covered the turning of the bathroom door's metal knob.

Her hand grabbed the soap just as his reached to pull open the shower's translucent plexi-glass door.

Wham!

The front door to the apartment thundered open.

From the shower, Kelly heard her name being shouted at the top of someone's lungs! "*Kelly! Kelly!*" She pushed the plastic knob down, opened the shower door, grabbed her robe hanging on a hook on the back of the bathroom door and slipped it on a split second before Ken burst into the bathroom.

"You okay?" he yelled, breathless.

"What the hell you think you're doing?" Kelly was shocked by his sudden, yelling appearance! And in her bathroom!

"Check the back," Ken yelled to Chuck. "I've got this side."

The two detectives split up, rushing to check each of the rooms in the apartment, running to do so without giving Kelly any explanation.

"You can't just barge in here like this!" she ranted, trooping after them from room-to-room. "This place isn't even mine! Look what you've done to the front door."

Ken stopped searching only long enough to inform her, "We thought you were in danger."

Chuck returned to the living room.

"All clear."

Perturbed, she pulled the robe more tightly around her. "I'm not in any danger...except from you guys."

Chuck grinned, stupidly saying, "You should put

on some clothes or you're in danger of catching a bad cold." Later in the squad car, he'd sputter to Ken some piss-ass excuse for why he had said that. "Cut me some slack, man!" After all, what else could a brother say after they both broke down the apartment's front door, ran fucking wild banshees through the entire place, room-to-room, trying to be Rambo's, finding nothing, and coming across like two bozos caught with their pants down? His grin turned to a nervous laugh.

"It's not funny." She belted the detective in the stomach, hard.

"You're right," Ken sounded apologetic, "but we got a message from the killer." He held up the print-out. "He said you were next. We got over here as soon as we could."

Pissed at the killer's giving them the run-around, Ken threw the print-out down on the couch.

"He got us again, chasing our tails."

Recovering from Kelly's punch to his gut, he said to her, "We were here to save you, you know."

"You were?" Kelly didn't know whether to laugh, thank them both for their caring or tell them to wait a few minutes 'til she finished her shower. That way picking up their trail would be a lot easier. The three of them could leave this place together: they in front, she behind.

"Yeah, we were," Ken supported his partner with the truth.

"Okay. Do me a favor, will you?"

"Sure," from the both of them.

"Knock next time." Then, deciding she'd rather enjoy trying to pick up their trail than the easy way out: going with them now, "Now, get the hell out of here."

"You sure you're okay?" Ken sounded concerned.

"Yeah, I'm sure." she replied, making light of a tough situation. "Nothing a good locksmith can't fix."

Chuck checked the door. It still opened and closed. "It's okay." He tried the lock. "Still locks. Well, we'd love to stick around, but we gotta get going. Right, Ken?"

"You got my pager number?" Ken said to Kelly, trying to sound not worried.

"Yes, Uncle Ken. I have all your numbers."

Ken nodded, and with that, the embarrassed duo left.

She closed the door behind them and headed back toward the shower, slipping off the robe as she entered.

Snap.

He grabbed her from behind just as she walked through the bathroom door. He forced her naked back against the wall, turning her around as he pushed her back. He rammed his body against hers.

Rock against velvet.

She screamed, backhanding him.

Her aggression and her trying to pull away excited him.

Great!

A challenge!

She pushed him off her bare breasts. She went for the door, which he slammed shut before she got through. He pulled her down. His maleness hot, surging, ready. One kind of pleasure before the ultimate!

He jammed his lips against hers. His hands reached to unzip his fly.

She shook her head, sideways. At the same time, she kneed him.

He flew backward, hurting. She got to the door, pulled it open. From behind, he grabbed her hair, yanking her head back.

Her right hand shot back, grabbed his wrist. She

pushed his wrenched wrist back as hard as she could. *The bitch had strength.* She whirled around and grabbed his thumb, pushing backward, with all her might toward his wrist, a move her father had taught her when she wasn't even 10. His hand seared in agony! Pain sliced up his arm. *The bitch wants a fight! She'll get*—his right foot flew up and around, sweeping and shoving her off him. She fell to the floor. He jumped on top of her, straddling her, eager, coming down, ready to thrust.

Her fingers clawed his fly and her bare legs clamped shut! So fast, so tight, so unexpectedly—he's caught! Clamped in the steel gripping jaws of self preservation.

He smashed her across the face. She clamped tighter! A bullet of pain shot upward from his pulsing organ! His right index and middle finger shot out and spear-handed her in the eyes.

She screamed. Her clamp opened!

⌣·

"I can't believe I left the print-out behind."

"No shit, Ken." Chuck was disgusted. "It's evidence."

The two turned, walked back up the two flights of stairs to Kelly's temporary home. In front of the door, Ken reached for the knob, ready to enter unannounced.

"Eh, eh, eh," Chuck clucked. "I wouldn't do that. We gotta knock first."

"Right." Ken knocked lightly.

No answer.

Inside, almost blinded, she ran toward the kitchen. Her hands fumbling around, pulling drawers open, looking for a knife.

He was on her, behind her.

She sent an elbow extension into his face. He grabbed her other arm and spun her around, knocking the kitchen table off balance. It crashed to the floor.

The sound sent Ken crashing through the front door. He saw Kelly being thrust up against the refrigerator. He lunged toward the intruder he knew was the killer and slammed the ball of his foot into the killer's back.

The killer spun around, leaping and knife handing O'Hara while Kelly ran from the kitchen into Chuck's arms in the living room. Ken stepped back, and in his step backward, the killer took the advantage and ran.

Out of the kitchen, through the hallway and toward the bedroom and the window he had left open when he had entered.

Ken chased the killer, a raging bull. That son of a bitch killer had tried to hurt his family!

The killer leaped through the window, out onto the fire escape.

Ken leaped right behind him.

The killer took the steps, three, four, five at a time, running down the black metal, Ken close on his heels.

On a landing, the killer suddenly turned. He shot a powerful kick upward, connecting with a running Ken. Ken fell backward. His legs slid through the fire escape. His hands grasped the thin railing.

The killer ran up the steps, pulling his heavy-booted foot back, getting ready to punt Ken's fingers grasping the rail.

Ken swung his legs upward, under and through the railing just as the killer punted—and missed. Ken leaped onto his assailant, smashing the killer's back up against the rail.

The killer loved the feel of the rail across his back and O'Hara standing over him! He was trapped! Like a fox, it's leg clamped between two clasping metal jaws! With the trapper about to bash its head in with a rifle! The killer got a rush!

He raised his leg and with his the thick cleated heel of his boot jabbed Ken in the abdomen, the soft underbelly just above the groin. Ken threw a fist into the killer's face. The killer turned; Ken's fist smashed into the building's brick wall.

The killer back-fisted Ken's face up against the wall. He heard the sound of flesh grinding against brick as he whipped the cop's face back-and-forth. Another rush.

Enjoying himself too much to end it, the killer let go and ran down two more flights of metal stairs.

Assuring himself Kelly was okay, Chuck had run to the bedroom window the killer had obviously used to enter the apartment. He stepped out onto the seventh floor fire escape landing. The killer was four floors below him. Or more. He raised his gun and squeezed off a few shots. None hit.

The killer jumped through the closed window, landing inside an empty bedroom. He ran for the bedroom door.

Ken jumped through the window and ran toward the killer, who was now racing through the vacated apartment. The killer kicked open the door leading to the hallway and ran down the third-floor hallway. Close on his heels was Ken.

In the hallway, the killer grabbed a potted fake tree standing outside a locked apartment door. He picked up the cement pot and threw it back at Ken, who ducked just as the killer kicked open another locked apartment door, ran toward a window and, without concern, leaped through the closed window, shattering the window into hundreds of pieces of glass. He leaped down onto the roof of a moving truck.

Right behind ran the killer, his mind pumping, "No retreat in battle!"

Seeing Kelly pushed up against the refrigerator, screaming, he leaped through the window after the bastard. Landing on the same moving truck.

The killer bludgeoned Ken with his fists, sneering, "It's not your time yet, Detective O'Hara," and side-kicking the cop off the truck's roof, onto the street.

Ken's body tossed off the truck by the rapid powerful kick sent shoppers on the street hurling themselves into shop doors or up against building walls. Ken's body hit and bounced off the hood of a taxi stopped at a red light.

The taxi driver stuck his head out, cursed and yelled in broken English, "Hey, man, what'ta fuck you! I gotta a fare! Get the fuck off!"

The driver stepped on the gas, then the brake, jerking Ken off his taxi, explaining to the stunned Japanese tourists in the back seat, "Fucking New Yorkers, they do damned near anything to get a cab."

One of the tourists reacted quickly, turning and snapping a Kodak moment of Ken lying flat on his back in the middle of the street to impress the folks back home how American businessmen have to fight to stay ahead.

A cop working traffic at the intersection rushed to assist the body lying on the street.

Moments later, Chuck appeared. He helped Ken to sit on a nearby stoop and delivered the bad news.

"He's gone."

Ken, feeling very bruised and the center of unwanted attention, delivered more news.

"He could've killed me. Said it wasn't my time."

Chapter 13

Justice finished tinkering with Chuck's PC in his office. "I loaded it in there for ya, Detective."

"What commands?" Burke eagerly asked the hacker-turned-installer wanting to make a quick exit from the station he didn't feel comfortable in. Even if he was helping out the police.

Justice pointed to a series of keys, then hit "enter."

"Hope it makes you happy." The station's computer jumped to react. Booting up, "Ooh, just for you!" teasingly through the speaker as Justice turned, he got an eyeful and asked, "Who's the babe?"

Burke stared at the screen.

"What a babe! She comes immediately upon that command, Justice?" It'd been a long time since Burke had felt so tingly all over. Then he felt guilty, condemning himself for letting himself get so excited by a graphic! But what a graphic! Better than most real life; at least, most of his real life.

"Kelly!" Ken said, turning to respond to Justice's question. "What are you doing here?" She was walking—alone—straight toward the two detectives who from their appearance to her were playing computer games. "Where's the uniform assigned to protect you?" Ken asked.

Kelly, smartly dressed in tight jeans and a black leotard top, a thin blouse hanging open over the tight top, didn't answer Ken's question. She informed him, "I'm working on this case with you, Ken. If I'm a target, where would I be safer than with you two? Take me along or I'll just keep following you 'til you do. You know that, Uncle Ken."

Burke fumbled to hit any key to get rid of Miss "Just for you!" He whirled around, the quick turn turning him from voyeur back to detective, shyly grinning, a kid caught with his hand in the cookie jar.

"She's got a point, Ken. She's a target now."

What could Ken say except, "Promise to stay out of our way?"

"You got it, Uncle Ken."

Chuck tried to be businesslike

"Promise you won't ever call me Uncle Chuck?"

She nodded.

"Then, welcome onboard!" Chuck shot out his hand, which she shook while Ken just shook his head and Justice gingerly took his leave.

The next week went by with nothing from the killer. No e-mail. No graphics. No on-line video feed. No killings Nothing.

The detective duo, now a trio, slogged their way through blind lead after blind lead, returning to crime scenes, comparing police photos to the actual place of incident.

They had the department artist sketch a portrait from Chuck, Ken and Kelly's descriptions. Showing this pencil drawing around the Lower East Side. Nothing. Not even from paid informants.

The three had the chief haul in a van-load of pimps, streetwalkers and other assorted low life.

Nothing.

Of course, they had very little to go on when questioning the street vermin about other street offal.

The three visited martial arts studios from Times Square, 42nd Street south and east to the Holland Tunnel. The killer—so skilled in various martial arts techniques—had to have been someone's student. But apparently he never studied in NYC. But they still hadn't checked out the Bronx, Brooklyn, Long or Staten Island. That could take forever. Time they didn't feel they had.

"He didn't spring from nowhere!" Ken kept arguing every time Kelly and Chuck wanted to quit after visiting—how many was it now, a hundred martial arts studios? "Make that a hundred and ten."

"This guy had to have trained somewhere. He's too good."

"No instructor teaches killing people," Chuck reminded Ken. "Goes against everything in martial arts philosophy. Respect for life and all."

Ken wouldn't be placated.

"This killer's been testing killing methods," he was theorizing. "We believe martial arts' effectiveness; this killer's actually trying it out."

"And I'm on his list of those he's trying his methods out on," Kelly stated, "that it?"

Ken nodded, adding, "I've got the feeling he's almost done. I just wish we knew who was next."

"Don't we all?" Chuck pulled a coin out of the air, back to doing magic to amuse his friends "here" in NYC in a little hole-in-the-wall bar while they were having a night-time, off-hours drink together, not in a dive in "Atlantic City." Not yet, anyway!

Kelly excused herself to go to the john.

"Why'd you quit, Ken?" Chuck asked, palming the coin.

Ken went silent. He hadn't wanted to quit. He was trained never to quit. But "I was working serials, like you." Ken resigned himself to telling his story, the first time to anyone else except Megan. "I tracked the bastard ped, got inside his head. He had killed ten by then, and I took him down. But I had seen too much, done too much. I just never wanted to experience that kind of evil again. I didn't want it in my life."

"He hurt you, right?"

"Almost killed me." Ken's mind flew back to that night he was hanging from the warehouse girders. The taut wires cut into his wrists. Every movement, even his slightest movement, bit the wires more deeply into his flesh.

The snapping whip slashed and peeled the skin off his back. He felt it now, sitting in this bar. The whip's snapping, his involuntary reaction digging the wires deeper, into the bone. His wrists wrenched in pain as he grasped his beer more tightly.

"Killed my marriage, too," Ken was right on with this one. "I'm trying to salvage it, but—you saw for yourself."

Chuck felt for Ken. He could empathize. He was.

"I was married...long time ago. When I was in the academy. It ended badly, and I blamed it on the job, but that wasn't it. I just didn't try hard enough."

"Too bad."

"I don't know much about you, Ken, but you don't seem like the kind of guy to give up. Am I right?"

"Yeah," Ken wanted to believe that about himself.

"I guess."

"Then you shouldn't give up on your marriage, man. To this day, my only regret is that I didn't save my marriage when I could have. All I had to do was call her."

Ken knew it was coming.

"All you have to do is call her."

He reacted quickly, defensively.

"How'd this parable about you suddenly get about me?"

"The moral of the story is," Chuck was becoming a pain in the ass, "just give her a call. See if you can save it. You got the chance—take it."

Ken hesitated and took a sip of his beer. He looked around the bar, wishing Kelly would get back. Her presence would end this do-gooder analysis/advice session. She didn't come back. Musta had to wait. This place didn't have toilet parity, obviously. He had to say something. So, to shut Burke up, "Maybe I will."

Triggering Burke's immediate response, "You've got motive, and you've got opportunity." He pointed to two phones along the back wall. They were not in use.

"You know nothing about me," Ken tried to fight back.

"Don't want to know anymore, pal." Chuck pulled a quarter from the air near Ken's ear. "Here's a quarter. If it lands heads, you call her. Deal?"

What could he do?

"Deal."

Chuck flipped, careful to keep the coin covered and flipped away from Ken and with a magician's quick sleight of hand so his partner'd never see both sides of the trick coin were heads!

Without another word, Ken headed toward the phone, just as Kelly was coming out of the women's room.

Chapter 14

Cool summer evening's breezes brushed against their hands

clasped together as they walked the newly-constructed Riverfront Mall. Thanks to Trump, tiny shops, lit up like Christmas, twinkling in the onslaught of an orange sunset. To the east, a bright big moon was rising over the horizon, peeking through the towering spires. Redder than usual.

The day had been much more fun than he had ever expected. The truth be known: they had both been hungering for such a day. A long time.

"You seem different, Ken." Megan wasn't just making conversation.

Well, maybe not different, she thought for a moment, then certain, "More like the old Ken."

"You mean the 'young' Ken," he laughed. Remembering a time way, way back in high school, when being together was great fun, when life didn't have jobs and responsibilities and mortgage payments and serial killers. Damn, why didn't life ever stay that way? He had busted his butt to build self-confidence. He had pulled his way from being a gangly "Mantis" in elementary school to a fairly decently respected average kid in junior high, then onto a popular BMOC in high school. Even in college. What a metamorphosis!

That didn't stop.

With reckless abandon, he had morphed himself into a mindhunter, a final change that had reduced Megan to living in constant fear. Except for maybe today. But he wasn't tracking anyone today. He was looking for something: a way to bring his marriage back together again, to rebuild his home. Give Lauren a mommy and daddy—together—again. Give himself a life that now only felt half, almost voided.

Megan saw a bench.

"Can we sit for a little while, please?"

He lead her toward the bench

"I'd like that."

The two sat in silence for what seemed like ten hours, neither knowing exactly what to say. Finally, Ken spoke.

"I know it's been tough, and—" Chuck had been right. "—I haven't been trying hard enough. I want to change that."

She leaned against him.

"You know it was never about my not loving you."

"I don't know how to explain it," Ken was searching for the right words. "I...I just shut off the world."

"You shut me out," Megan was quiet, gracious, truthful. He'd get going after a serial; the serial'd take over his entire being. Totally. Every waking moment. He'd become tight-lipped, not wanting to say anything to frighten her. But his not saying anything only made her even more frightened, her mind filling his silence with all kinds of horrible scenarios, every one ending with his violent death.

Not too long, his silence, her fear led to barely touching one another. Each felt the other—during sex—was jabbing for human contact yet not willing to give to get. "I can't, I refuse to live like that." Again, quiet, gracious, truthful, firm.

"It was the biggest mistake I ever made." Ken was saying what he wanted to say since five minutes after she walked out of their home. "I won't do that again. I need your support, all the time."

She turned into him.

"You have it. You always have."

He looked into her eyes, searching for a hint.

"So what do you say? Can we live together, a family?"

A tear filled her eye; his answer.

A tear filled his, the first she'd ever seen from him.

He pulled her into him. Close. They hugged, oblivious to the world around them as the sun sank lower and the moon rose higher, its red hue deepening as it shone down on them.

"How about moving back in this weekend?" he asked between kisses. "I'll try to free up this case to help."

"Lauren would love to move back home." Megan laid her head on his chest. Again, she was truthful.

"How about you?"

She looked up into his eyes.

"Me too."

They kissed, the moment bridging years of heartache, bringing two people together.

Interrupted by his beeper!

"Damn!" He wanted to trash the buzzing symbol of

his life in the Hudson.

"Comes with the territory." She was honest. Yet somehow her tone just now and her gentle touch to his neck seemed different, like the "old" Megan. No, like the "young" Megan.

He clicked off the beeper.

"Better answer this." He glanced at the pager's message, then to her. "This weekend?" he said hopefully.

"This weekend," she nodded. He kissed her again, then headed toward a phone to call in. She whispered, lovingly, "Be careful."

"You got it!" he called back, almost skipping to a phone mounted on the wall of the tiny Christmas village shop.

Chapter 15

Ken flew in his Honda, Chuck on his Triumph and Kelly in her Accord, each arriving at the crime scene at about the same time.

They made their way through the gaggle of police and rescue crew standing around, waiting for official word on what to do next.

"Talk to me. Talk to me," Chuck issued an order as he moved toward the dead body lying on the dance club floor covered by a sheet pulled from the ambulance.

"Another one, Detective. Burke," the shield standing near the corpse said. "No weapons, no prints, no witnesses. Nothing."

Neither Chuck, Ken, nor Kelly needed to be told. This was victim seven. Same MO, same signature.

"There's something written on the floor," the shield said to all three. "I couldn't make it out." The cop pointed toward the wood floor close to the victim's hand.

Faint, barely readable, small drops of blood. Or was it a line? You'd have to strain belief to think this was writing. Or anything other than splatter. Yet the victim's right index fingertip was covered with dried blood. So, maybe—

"Can you read it?" Chuck asked a stooping, examining Ken.

"No. You?"

Chuck got down as close to the floor and the blood drippings as possible. A few moments later, having squinted and turned every which way he could trying to make out something, "I don't know...might be a 'C' and an 'A' and maybe—"

Ken motioned the department photographer toward Chuck who, standing up, ordered the photographer to "get some good shots of this and blow them up for me, okay?"

Flashes popped immediately.

While Ken and Chuck hovered near the dead body, Kelly moved around the dance club room. Not trained in investigative techniques, she relied on female instincts. What didn't look right? What could she find? What'd her gut tell her. Bingo! She noticed an empty picture frame on the floor.

Odd.

She bent down and, wearing tight latex gloves, picked up the frame. Nothing unusual. Except no picture. Maybe some new kind of themed decoration for the club. These days people were earning big money decorating clubs and restaurants with junk and cast-offs. But an empty picture frame on the floor? Oh, well, who knows?

Nah, it must have fallen from the wall.

She looked closely at the wall just above where the picture lie on the floor and thought she saw a lighter area. Or was it dustier? Or less dusty? She couldn't tell where the picture might have hung. A closer look, and she saw some blood on the wall, right beside the hook on which the picture frame must have hung.

"What do you make of this?" she said loudly enough for Chuck to hear. "There's blood on the wall?"

Chuck walked over to Kelly. He saw the empty picture frame in her hand.

"Hmm, the mystery picture. Who do you think is in it?"

Ken, still standing beside the shooting photographer, read Chuck's look.

"Get a shot of the wall, and as soon as this scene is processed, get these pictures over to the office, too, okay?" Then he walked to Kelly, complimenting her snooping skills. "You did good, Kelly."

But "doing good" wasn't nailing her father's killer. Or making her feel any safer.

Back at the station, the crime scene pic blow up showed the letters "C-H-A." On a white board in Chuck's office, Ken and Kelly were writing down every "Cha" word they could think of. The list read:

Chamberlain
Chambers
Chambless
Champs
Chammon
Chasson
Chassen
Chanting
Chatterly
Chance

"I tell you," Chuck observed the list, "he's trying to write the killer's name."

"Why a name?" Ken asked.

"Why would a dying body write 'champagne'?"

Even Ken had to admit Chuck had a point.

"Maybe it's not a name," Kelly countered. "Maybe it's a 'something.' Like chamber, chamberlain, chambermaid, I don't know."

Ken snickered

"Yeah, Miss Marple, the chambermaid did it."

Nobody laughed. Who was Miss Marple?

Kelly kept reeling off possible somethings: Chamber music, chambray, chameleon, chamfer, chaoisa, chamomile— Ken and Chuck looked at Kelly, a bit incredulously. She only shrugged.

"So I was good at Scrabble! That and I always tested my Reader's Digest Word Power." She continued showing off her word skills: Champ—champion—

"Hey, wait a minute!" A light dawned inside his head.

"Champion!" Ditto Chuck's. "Son of a bitch!"

"It was right here the whole time," Ken stated, feeling down on himself for not realizing long, long before this.

"What?" Kelly asked.

"All the victims were or are champions," Chuck said. Ken nodded his agreement. "He's killing them all."

As if one person suddenly thinking alike and at the same time, Ken and Chuck quickly moved toward the bulletin board. They looked at the photos of each dead body. "Boxing. Wrestling. Tough Man. Karate. Kendo. Kickboxing. Shit!" Chuck pointed to each photo.

"These are all champions, but they wouldn't have fought each other. They have their own competitions."

Ken strained his memory. Where had he seen all these champions pictured together before? And when? Slowly, it came into view in his mind.

"They fought together once."

"Huh?" from Chuck.

"Yeah," Ken was becoming more and more certain, "and the link is her father, my instructor."

"What are you talking about?" Chuck was getting impatient.

"Ever hear of The Master's Challenge?"

"Damn!" Chuck knew where Ken was going.

"The tag line was—"

"Tournament of Champions," Kelly finished the nationwide slogan branded on everything: T-shirts, mugs, postcards, anything marketable, wearable, or take-homeable.

"I've got some magazines with those pictures in it," Chuck was getting excited. Maybe he'd soon have something for the chief.

Chuck pulled the bottom desk drawer out and grabbed a magazine. He quickly paged through it.

"Here it is!"

"That's it!" Kelly shouted. "This is the photo from The Master's Challenge."

"Recognize anyone?" Chuck asked both his colleagues.

"Yeah." Ken became somber. "Most of them are staring at steel, in drawers at the morgue. Think our boy is in the picture?"

The trio looked from face-to-face. Eddie Cunningham, boxer. Victim.

Dutch Schultz, tough man. Victim. Kurt McKinney, point Karate. Victim. Mark Cramer, kickboxing, victim. Master Welling, master instructor. Victim. Kevin Haley, Judo, most recent victim.

"Who're these two guys?" Ken pointed to two handsome young faces.

"The first guy," Chuck pointed to a black-haired

stud, then ran his finger down to the caption, "is Chad Atkins."

"Who's he?" Kelly asked.

Chuck ran his finger down through the article accompanying the picture, speed-reading. "Hmm—kung fu stylist," he began picking out words, "disqualified during the Tournament of Champions for excessive contact—broke one competitor's ribs."

"I like him so far," Ken whistled.

Chuck went to his PC, tied into the station's system, typed in "Chad Atkins." A blip, a whirling clicking, and info starting appearing on screen: "Atkins, Chad, DOA, Presbyterian Hospital. Cause of death: automobile accident. Date: Sept. 1, 1994."

"Shit!" Ken didn't mask his disappointment.

"Of the remaining two in the picture, one is dead," Chuck repeated. "Car crash, confirmed."

"That leaves this guy. Willie Namath." Ken was reading names in the caption, searching for words in the article. "He fits the profile—age, height and weight. Kelly, you recognize him?"

"No!" she shook her head. "He was on me too fast. I don't—"

"This Namath guy has a sheet you wouldn't believe," Chuck was reading the computer's screen. "Picked up a bunch of times for assault. Did time for assault with intent to kill."

"No model citizen," Ken observed, matter-of-factly.

"It gets worse," Chuck continued reading the screen. "We had him here last month on something related. Couldn't hold him—"

"I'm liking this guy more than Atkins," Ken was thinking.

"Atkins' dead," Chuck reminded his partner of the obvious.

"And Namath's got a wrap sheet for assault—" Ken was trying to picture the guy in the magazine picture with much longer hair and a bronzed, deeper skin color. Not exactly a perfect match, but with two years or so since the picture had been taken, maybe—

"Let's send a strike team out after him."

"We're on it!" Chuck agreed. He buzzed Margie, asking her to alert the chief of what was coming down. Then he was out his office door, Ken by his side, both followed by Kelly.

Downstairs, in the garage, Ken and Chuck hopped into their squad car, Kelly right behind them eagerly

"Do I get a gun?"

"Sorry, Kelly. You can't go along." Ken was firm. "You'll have to stay here until we find this guy."

"You said yourself I was safer with you two!" Kelly protested.

"I agreed when you said that," Ken corrected her statement.

"We're walking into the valley of the shadow of death here, Kelly," Chuck opened the car's door, driver's side. "We won't be able to protect you."

"When have you ever?" she shot back.

"Discussion's over." Ken got into the car. "Decision's been made. It's for your own good, Kell."

"Right!" she stormed. "That must be why I feel so good."

"Let's go!" Ken slammed his door shut, locking out the fuming Kelly.

Moments later, the SWAT team in place, Ken and Chuck double-timed to the front door.

Storming the Bastille.

Chuck drew his automatic.

"You've got the gun," Ken whispered. "You go in

first. Let's stop this psycho!"

Weapon drawn, Chuck kicked the door open and jumped into the room, scanning the room with his eyes and gun.

Nothing.

Ken followed directly behind his partner. He motioned Chuck to go one way, he'd go the other.

Ken checked the living room.

Nothing.

Chuck scanned the kitchen.

Nothing.

Ken moved down the hallway and threw open a door. An office of sorts. Nothing out of the ordinary. A desk. A computer. A trash can.

Nothing.

Chuck met Ken in the middle of the house. He motioned toward a door they both supposed led to the basement. They nodded. *We're going through.*

A million miles away, Megan pulled the U-Haul up to Ken's home, about to be hers and Lauren's once again.

"We really going home?" Lauren had asked all day.

And every time she'd be asked the question, Megan would nod, assuring the hopeful child, "Yes, we really are."

And to every "Yes, we really are," Lauren would beg to know, "For real?"

"For real."

"Promise?"

"Promise."

"Daddy know this?"

"He asked us to come back."

"He never wanted us to leave."

Truth from the mouth of a child.

"So now we're back!" Megan said, unlocking the

door and stepping inside. "Home."

"For good?" Lauren didn't enter until Megan nodded assuringly, "For good."

"Let's call Daddy. Let him know."

"He's at work."

"This he'd want to know."

Again, more truth from a child.

Megan dialed Ken's pager number.

Bzzzt!

As they walked down the steps, Chuck's gun drawn, Ken's attention focused on the still darkness in front of them, the pager sounded like a giant buzzing alarm!

Quickly, someone leaped out of the darkness, kicking both men in their shins. Chuck fired.

The SWAT team came running down the cellar steps! A moment later, the attacker from the dark was beaten down, handcuffed and wounded slightly.

"Thanks, guys," Chuck looked up at the helmeted cops still scrambling down the steps. "I think we can take care of it from here."

Chapter 16

Kelly felt very alone. Her father had been taken from her so ruthlessly. One moment he was standing on the training floor cheering her on, the next he was felled to that same floor, savagely brutalized and murdered by some whacko fiend. And those two! Maybe she didn't have all the strength in the world, but she could hold her own. Against most anyone. And if that "anyone" was her father's killer, she'd find all the power in the world inside herself to pound that destroyer of her whole life into the ground, her payback.

But no. She shucked off at that moment the killer's possible apprehension. Shoved aside and shelved like a rag doll tossed into the trash, a plaything pitched to the dump when no longer needed or wanted. Without even a moment's thought given to her feelings. This was her father that killer had savagely mangled and mutilated, stomped on 'til he was dead. That was her home that bastard had violated. Her entire life that son of a bitch serial had shit upon! Didn't those very reasons count for something on why she should be allowed to share the final moment of the killer's capture and their victory? Fucking A! Is this how women feel allowed—no, encouraged—to haul ass in the army, navy and whatever, to train like freaking mudrats, to endure men's farting lewd crassness every day of their duly enlisted lives while pulling their own weight every step of the way, only to be denied entrance into combat, the whole reason they'd entered and endured training in the first place!

Life wasn't fair. But her father had told her that. Years ago.

Back then, she was hiding in the corner, way, way in the back of the dojo, almost not even standing on the training floor. Moments before, he had demonstrated a very basic kick: up, out and snap, then back. This technique, an individual move, was foundational.

She was awed watching her father whenever he taught martial arts. She loved watching his chiseled body turning slightly to the left while throwing his muscular right leg up, very high into the air! "Wow! Straight up!" she'd squeal. And he did it again and again: up, out and snap, then back. His leg extension fast, fluid, natural; his bare foot snapping so quickly, so powerfully, she almost couldn't see it so fast it was!

But try as she might, she couldn't get the technique. She struggled to get her leg up and turn her body and stay on her feet, all at the same time. She'd lift, try to kick, wobble and fall. She'd fallen so many times, her backside hurt.

Up again, lifting, kicking, losing her balance, wobbling, and—ouch!— down!

Her father had left his twenty other students, all belt levels, to come to assist her. "Kelly," he squatted down on his haunches, looking into his tiny daughter's eyes,

"It's tough, isn't it?"

She dropped her head and fought back a tear, feeling humiliated in front of the others, mostly teenage boys and young men. She tried not to say the forbidden words, but she just had to, not looking up at him, admitting to all the world, "I—can't—sir."

Her father, now her master instructor, put her hand underneath Kelly's chin and lifted her face and eyes up to look into his. "Never say, 'I can't.'" He was firm but spoke quietly so no one else would hear. Not like a drill sergeant. Not like a father. Like a potter sculpting clay, careful to mold the finest of products.

"But I tried," she meekly tried to defend herself.

"Keep trying," he encouraged the child. "I'll help you." He pointed to the six-year-old's right leg, instructing, "Tighten this leg and put most of your weight on that leg. Fighter's stance."

Kelly did so.

"Now let your other leg hang loose," he said, positioning himself close behind the child as she tried to let her other leg hang loose.

She really tried, shaking her leg trying to force it to hang loose, then hitting her leg to get it to hang loose.

"Relax, Kelly, relax," he encouraged her as he bent down, grasped her ankle, wiggled and shook the tension out of her taut little leg muscles. As he did so, he looked up into his daughter's eyes and whispered a secret meant only for the two of them: "It's okay to fall. As many times as it takes." Then, even quieter, as if an even deeper secret: "I fell 'til I learned, too."

"You did, Daddy?!" her eyes widened in amazement. Her "example person" had fallen when he was learning, too!

"Fifty times," he winked.

"That many times!" Her mouth dropped open.

He nodded.

"That many times."

If he fell, she thought, So can I— and she swung her foot loosely, lifted her leg higher than she thought ever possible, extended—a little wobbly—and snapped! *"I Can! I Can!"* She was ecstatic and never knew, not 'til years and years later when she passed her black belt test, her father's hand had helped her loose leg kick, extend, snap and come back to the floor.

That was the kind of man he was. Tough as nails to those he believed in, using whatever worked—setting an almost impossibly high standard to be attained, cajoling and wheedling to keep trying, threatening no longer to be their instructor! Whatever worked to discipline their potential into the finest development.

And now he was gone.

Obliterated!

Why? Why? Why?

Because he was the instructor who demanded only the best? Or had he somehow called the bluff of that Chad Atkins who'd been disqualified at the Tournament of Champions? Had Master Wayne Welling, her father, stripped away that Chad Atkins' tough he-man, martial arts warrior exterior to reveal the truth: that he was only a hollow shell with an empty spirit more interested in hurting than in respecting life?

Wait a minute! Chad Atkins was dead!

If he was dead, what was he doing walking into the Chameleon Club right now?!

The metal detector's distinctive beep had broken her reverie into her past. She looked up to see what was causing the sound and saw Chad Atkins—from the picture!

But Chuck's computer had said he was dead.

Yet there he was, his metal-tipped fingers setting off the metal detector! And there she was, sitting in the club seeing—was it her attacker?—and—could it be? the first two fingers on his right hand were metal? *Fierce looking rods of steel*, she thought.

He pulled his metal fingers back through the security machine and barreled his way through the machine.

The bouncer stepped in front of him, blocking his entrance into the club. She watched in horror—not believing her eyes—as Atkins slammed his two metal rods into the bouncer's right eye and temple. The next second he was enjoying the thrill of pushing his self-designed, home-made special weapon into the bouncer's skull. After he had been disqualified from the Tournament of Champions, he had made up his mind. No one would ever disqualify him from anything ever again! He was just as good—no, he was better, much, much fucking better than any of those so-called "champions."

Champions of what? They'd never fought him! So, at the most, any—no all—of those bums claiming to be a "world champion" were, in reality, also-rans! Runner-ups! He was the "*Champion!*" They were losers. All of them.

Or soon would be.

For good.

Especially when he hit them with his home-made fist! Late one night he had hit upon the idea: a weapon to end all weapons! He drank himself almost into a stupor. Beginning with a six-pack of Coors, which he thoroughly enjoyed, slopping it down while watching Jackie Chan movies, laughing, burping and farting to his heart's content, then guzzling the pint or so of gin he'd had around his dojo and finding himself really looking forward to downing some whiskey or vodka. Ah, that night's drinking bout made his good old college days seem really very, very Cinderella. Not tonight!

He never made it to hitting the whiskey or vodka because mid-way through the third Jackie Chan movie, he was ready.

He went out into his kitchen, which he always kept amazingly neat, spotless, devoid of even the slightest piece of garbage, not even a tiny sliver of twisted wax paper, foil or paper towel. He grabbed a butcher knife and in one whack, lopped off the first two fingers on his right hand.

A month later, though his nubs were still tender, he forced onto each a stainless steel tube, which he had fashioned into vicious sharp claws, so sharp that he cut slice a tissue in mid air as it floated downward, now in two neatly-cut pieces.

He had first experimented on rats, throwing the rodents into the air, flicking his claws, and, in a split, clean, slicing second, two hind legs and a tail fell to his linoleum kitchen floor a second before a head and two front legs plopped downward into a bloody splat. "Cool!" He was thrilled. But much moreso the morning he threw a young collie pup upward toward his kitchen ceiling and, in lightning punches, punctured its stomach, lungs, eyes and nose before skewering its anus shish kebab-style.

So no piss-ass bouncer was going to stand in his way. Not tonight!

As he pushed the bouncer aside, his eyes met hers. Each recognized the other!

The killer moved toward Kelly quickly. His hands were already tightening in eager anticipation of her supple body within his grasp, pulling her ass into his crotch, then maybe pushing her beneath himself, then—well, then, who knows?

But no matter what, tonight, this time, she'd be his. Wholly his.

Frantic, but determined to keep her cool, Kelly saw him moving toward her, and in one quick move jumped up and hurriedly entered the frenzied dancing bodies packed side-by-side on the dance floor.

A second later and on the floor, she gyrated with this guy, quickly slid two feet across the floor and did the macarena with that guy, then, even more quickly, hopped under that guy's upward extended arm and twirled around twice with a hefty 230-pounder out on the town and looking for some yum-yum. Though his shaking, undulating bulk hid her from the killer's view, she wasn't about to turn this slobby hulk into a human shield. If she did, he'd be shredded in seconds.

The killer hurriedly joined the dance action, high-stepping from one group of sweaty dancers to another. Trying to work his way across the floor to her.

But before he'd gotten to her, the music ended. The dancers milled around and wandered off the floor. Except him. The killer looked around the empty dance floor.

Kelly was gone.

The killer scanned the room. *The bitch was nowhere to be found.*

He hadn't expected to walk into this club tonight and suddenly hit paydirt! But now that he was here and now that she was here, he'd make good use of the time. He scanned the room again.

No Kelly.

Nowhere.

He shuffled quickly toward the women's room and stood there, waiting. For the moment. When no one entered or left the room for five minutes, he pushed the door open and went inside. No legs hanging down in any stall. Pissed, he pushed each stall's door open. Snapping his fingers together. Determined to find her if she was standing on a stool.

No Kelly.

Not in the women's room.

He was getting annoyed, getting the feeling his prey was somehow eluding him or playing with him. Snapping his fingers together, a hungry claw, he exited the women's room and scanned the dance club room again.

No Kelly.

"Damn! She must have gotten out!" His finger claw snapped as if punctuating his nonchalant, "Not to worry." He left, exiting through the emergency exit, setting off an alarm.

He ran through the parking lot.

No Kelly.

Angered that he was out-foxed again, he slammed a fist against his puke green Hugo, unlocked and yanked open the door, and tore out of the parking lot.

As soon as she could hear the killer putt-putt exiting the parking lot, she sat up in the driver's seat of her Accord, switched on the ignition, popped the car into gear and followed the killer, laughing up a storm. He may be up on the latest martial arts techniques, but this guy didn't know shit about cars!

⌣·

Riding in their squad car, returning to the station, Ken asked Chuck, "Seemed a little too easy, don't you think?" referring to their nabbing Willie Namath an hour ago.

"Much too easy," Chuck agreed. "The guy hardly fought back, and he certainly wasn't much of a fighter."

"What gives?" Ken asked the question more of himself than of Chuck. Was the killer about to sucker punch them both? Yet how could he? He was cuffed and on his way downtown. Or was he?

⌣·

She followed the killer to a public housing project. She guessed they were at about 125th Street though she didn't really know. She had kept her eyes glued to his rear end, not even looking up to glance at street signs as she sailed through intersections.

But the buildings had changed in appearance, from tall majestic, well-manicured hotels to boarded-up windows, graffiti-scrawled walls. And he was still driving north. Unaware he was being followed.

What a feeling! The huntress was enjoying the pursuit.

He was hers.

Hers without the two bozos to get in the way or take the credit.

How wrong they'd been to short circuit her burning desire to be there when they're grabbed the killer.

Wonder what ringer they found? she found herself asking herself as the Hugo pulled to the curb and to a stop. *Because they didn't get the killer.*

Chad Atkins jumped out of his car. He ran up to, then climbed, a stoop leading into a run-down apartment building in the project. He opened the door, and a moment later, the light went on in the first floor front window.

She opened her door and was about to step out of her car, into the street, when Atkins came barreling out the door and down the stoop. Reacting immediately, she pulled herself down behind her opened door and stayed cramped down until she heard the Hugo putt-putt off.

Then, cautiously, she raised her body and thus her head upward. She peeked just above the area where the door met the window. The Hugo and Atkins were definitely gone.

She made her move.

⌣·

"So who do you think we got?" Chuck asked Ken.

Ken didn't answer, too pissed off to speak. They'd been out-maneuvered again. But how? And by whom?

⌣·

Inside, she snooped around, looking for anything that might be considered evidence. She wasn't exactly certain what she was looking for, but that didn't stop her from stealthily entering every room, peeking into every closet, exploring every inch of what must be his home.

She went into his bedroom. Rather neat. Everything had its place, including the clothes in the closet: all neatly pressed, hanging in groupings—pants, shirts, jackets; the groupings arranged by color—black, charcoal, gray pants; black, magenta, purple shirts; two fleece jackets. Polished shoes, toes pointed inward away from the closet door, were on the floor beneath the hanging clothes. A basket of pressed boxers, socks and T-shirts beside the shoes. Joe-average dresser, she concluded.

She moved to a dresser pushed up against the wall. On top, several bottles of cologne, mostly musk and English Leather, were placed neatly side-by-side. She pulled open the top drawer and found several boxes of condoms. Even they were neatly set side-by-side.

Fastidious. the word popped into her mind as she looked around the room, everything in its place, everything so clean and neat, so incongruous with the neighborhood outside. *Oh, well,* she shrugged, not knowing why she kept thinking "fastidious" when she really wanted to say "obsessed."

She peeked into his bathroom. Might as well have been done as a showcase display for some interior decorator's home show somewhere. So neat, everything done in black-and-white, shower curtain black, tub white, shower rod off-white; track lighting—soft white bulbs in shiny black fixtures—emphasizing the wash bowl and the black-rimmed mirror which hung in such a way as to give a perfect view of the toilet when in full use; and, oh, yes, now that she was looking, even the toilet paper was fluffy white, resting neatly in a sparkling black holder. The roll's top sheet was folded neatly together in a triangle, motel-style when you first arrive in a just-cleaned room.

She crossed through the bedroom and entered a small alcove, the last room of her search for evidence which had thus far yielded only a "fastidious" black-and-white motif in the bathroom, and a mirror hung in an odd way near the black fur-trimmed off-white commode.

Then her eyes widened! Hung on each of the walls of the alcove: pictures of Cunningham, Schultz, her father, all dead; news clippings about the murders; a long list of—yes, his victims! And there, sitting on a neat, everything-in-its-place work station, a phenomenal computer system! As far as evidence goes, she'd found Fort Knox!

Ken's beeper cheeped as Chuck was pulling the squad car into the station garage. He looked down at the alphanumeric display printing out, "Found real killer. 123 Lynn Ave. I'm inside. Hurry. Kelly."

"Shit! Let's go!" he shouted to Chuck who slammed the car into reverse. The car shot backwards, straight out into the street.

Chuck yanked the wheel to the left, and the car jerked forward. He flicked on the siren, and they flew north.

"Well, Kelly, how nice to see you again."

She gasped!

He slammed the door to his alcove den shut tight.

"Have we...have we...met?" she stammered.

"Don't be coy." His fingers were itching for some

thumping action. Soon. "I've done some research on your career. You were a national champion, right?"

She focused on his clicking fingers.

"That's right."

"How interesting." He grinned.

Snap!

THWACK!

Chapter 17

Chuck and Ken's squad car careened around the corner. 132 Lynn!

Ken's door was open before the cruiser jerked to a stop. He was up the stoop before Chuck was out of the cop car. He had kicked in the front door just as Chuck reached his side, his gun drawn.

The door flew open, and Chuck swept the room with his gun.

Nothing.

Ken ran down the hallway, Chuck at his side.

Nothing.

Wait! What was that?

Ken stepped back, saw a blinking computer screen through a slightly-ajar door: City of New York Police Department System.

"No wonder he knew our every move," Ken cursed the computer as he stepped into the room. His eyes widened as he looked from wall-to-wall: newspaper clippings of the killings, pictures of the horribly wounded corpses the killer had apparently taken himself, and a list.

Ken moved closer to read the names on the list:
Eddie Cunningham
Dutch Schultz
Kurt McKinney
Mark Cramer
Wayne Welling
Kevin Haley
Kelly Welling
Ken O'Hara
Chuck Burke

Ken stepped closer to the wall to make certain his and Burke's names were indeed what he—

Thump!

His foot hit something beneath the computer workstation. He bent down, "Oh, shit! *No*!" he screamed, anger, vengeance, hatred, rage, all spewing pain.

"A lovely family you have, Ken," the computer suddenly came alive. A picture of Ken and Megan, obviously taken during an intimate moment on the Riverfront Mall, filled the screen, then supered over and, bleeding into the happy couple, Lauren. "Someone has to take care of your family, Ken."

Without a moment's hesitation, he grabbed a phone on the killer's workstation. He punched in numbers so fast the tones slid into one another.

Out on the island: "Hello?"

"Megan? Are you okay?"

"I'm fine. This is so like you, letting someone else do the dirty work."

"What are you talking about?"

"Your friend got here an hour ago, told me you couldn't get away, and helped me move everything in."

"What friend?" Ken grew silent for a moment. "Megan, listen to me. Where is he now?"

She noted the intensity of his silence.

"He's sitting next to Lauren. They're getting along—"

"If you can get away, do it. If not, don't let on anything's wrong, and I'll be there right away." Ken's tone was urgent, yet filled with love and a promise. "I won't let him hurt you, Megan. I love you."

She could barely speak.

"I'm scared, Ken."

"I know, baby. I'll be right there." He was quiet, firm, his firmness most reassuring.

"Don't hang up," Megan pleaded. "Let me call Lauren."

All Ken heard next was a loud scream and an even louder, "Mommy!" followed by a taunting, "Come for me, Ken. I'm waiting in the Forge. By the way, it's just us now, no one else. Just you two," the killer warned, looking at Megan and Lauren, "or they're dead."

He hung up.

"What's the Forge?" Chuck shouted to Ken's running back.

"It's a factory complex, deserted," Ken was almost out the front door and into the cruiser when he stopped, ran back into the house and den, grabbed the computer that had taunted him and threw it hard as he could to the floor.

"Ken, that's evidence!" Chuck shouted.

"There's not going to be a trial!" Ken retorted.

He was in the car, driver's side, yelling to Burke.

"He's taking them to the Forge!"

"Don't worry," Chuck said, sliding onto the passenger's seat, "we'll get them."

Ken started the car, slammed it into gear and tore off, warning his partner and boss, "I want to get something straight! I'm not looking to arrest this guy!" He flicked on the siren, hitting speeds upwards of 65, flying dangerously through intersections. "He came after my family; I'm going to kill him. You got a problem with that?"

Chuck looked at his partner—and friend—grimly. "I'm down with that."

Chapter 18

"No mercy."

"Loud and clear," Chuck confirmed Ken's call on this one, "boss."

Pulling an ancient sliding door open, its grating high-pitched screeching noises announcing the entrance of the detectives, Ken and Chuck stepped into the deserted building. What was once a factory was now an empty, black void. Suddenly, Ken saw himself stepping into another abandoned building. Like last time, Ken was closing in on a psycho serial. Also, like last time, he was unarmed. No weapons.

But this time, he was going after the gutless bastard who had just killed one of his family—Kelly's dead, savagely punctured, slashed face flew into his mind; he winced in pain—and now that same sadistic whacko monster held his wife and daughter captive somewhere in this cavernous blackness. And this time, though he carried no gun, he was armed to the hilt. With intense determination to bring down this serial.

Last time, that sicko serial ped had gotten to him,

wrecked havoc upon his life, ended his marriage, sent him into retirement. This time the tables were about to be turned. This vile killer would be his.

"Greetings, gentlemen!" The voice came out of nowhere. "You wouldn't shoot me in the back, would you?" The voice seemed disembodied, mechanic, meant to be disorienting to Ken and Chuck.

Both inched their way forward into the blackness.

As the voice continued, now from a different nowhere, "Especially when I am the only one who knows where Ken's lovely wife and daughter are."

And suddenly a laugh was everywhere! Pervading the cavernous blackness like poison circulating through the blood system.

Ken felt engulfed by this psycho's evil.

Then the building went silent.

Totally silent.

Ken strained to listen for the slightest sound, the least movement. Anywhere. None. Chuck, right beside him, kept his gun ready.

Ten minutes later, still total silence.

It frustrated Ken.

He touched his partner lightly on the arm. Together, they moved forward—slowly, very, very slowly, making no sound.

Snap.

Ken stopped. So did Burke.

Snap. Closer.

Ken tried to get a handle on that faint snapping sound. But before he could, the snap was beside him, laughingly jeering, "Welcome to hell."

"Where are they?" Ken turned and yelled toward the jeer in the blackness.

"I don't want them," the killer snickered. "I want"—

loudly licking his lips to unnerve the young detective—
"you."

"My wife and daughter, they aren't champions!"
Ken shouted back. In a flash he'd slam his foot into that
snickering snap if he knew what direction that fucking
clicking and snapping were coming from. "They are
innocent!"

"They are part of the plan, Ken," the killer rubbed
his fingers together, then became patronizing, as if talking to a small child, "Just like you and me."

"Your grand plan?" Ken asked, then taunted the hiding sneering killer. "Man, we figured you out long ago—
you couldn't hack it as a fighter, so you started killing
the real champions. The psychologist said something
about penis envy, didn't he, Chuck?"

"That was the complimentary part." Chuck's sarcasm infuriated the killer, who screamed, "Banter all
you want! The end game has begun." Suddenly whirling, slicing through a thick rope, sending a huge, con-
crete-filled barrel, tied off to the ceiling, crashing to the
floor, inches away from Ken and Chuck.

"Damn!" Chuck shouted. "That was too damn
close!"

A vicious pervading laugh.

Then the building fell silent.

Tired of playing this psycho serial's cat and mouse
game, Ken felt his way along the wall. The laugh had
seemed to come from above.

Another five steps and he felt a stairway leading
up. He tapped Chuck's shoulder: stay here; cover me.

Ken started climbing, jamming the front of his foot
up against the wooden step before stepping up. He
stepped up, then jammed his foot up against the wooden
step. He stepped up and felt for the next step.

It wasn't there. Some type of landing was.

With his right foot, he felt around. He took a step, then listened.

No sound other than Chuck's breathing down below him, becoming more and more anxious.

Ken took another step.

Wham!

He fell through a weakened, splintered floorboard. He thrust out his arms, catching himself from falling completely through the landing's floor. The splintered wood cut into his belly, slicing into his ribs.

A laugh everywhere.

"Ken!" Chuck yelled. "Ken, you okay?"

Before his partner could answer, Chuck was knocked to the ground.

Jumping from somewhere above the detective, the killer was on top of Burke. Then both were on the floor, Chuck on his back, the killer standing over him.

The killer whirled and shot a sidekick to Chuck's head. The force sent Chuck rolling over the floor, in pain. Still clutching his gun, he tried to get off a shot.

As if watching Chuck's action through night vision goggles, the killer did a high roundhouse kick, snapping his foot into the raised gun. The automatic skidded across the concrete floor.

Chuck pulled himself up, only to have the killer snap his heavily-booted foot into his face. Then Chuck felt himself being pulled by metal! He screamed! The two rods of pain were spears ramming into his skull, deadening his brain.

The killer laughed. *What could be more fun? His prey squealing in tormented anguish within his tightening grasp, this piss-ass detective writhing in pain, pleading for mercy. No challenge!* Shit, if this copper wasn't going to put up more of a fight, he might as well put this screaming bastard out of his misery. Now.

With his left hand, the killer grabbed Chuck by the hair, whipping the blacking-out detective's head upward, backward. He was about to thrust his home-made weapon into Chuck's bare forehead when—*oh, joy!*— he had a much, much better idea.

The killer held Chuck's head tight. Then relishing his idea, the thrill of the anticipated sound of cracking, breaking bones sending excited waves of intense eagerness running up and down his entire body, energizing him from the tip of his spine to the top of his head, then down into both arms. The killer grabbed Chuck's right arm, and in one quick upward thrust pulled, twisted and turned. What was more delightful to his ears? The sound of the bone breaking or the piteous scream of this worthless pile of shit? He couldn't decide. So, disgusted he couldn't decide, he threw the limp arm over the detective's head, useless. Maybe if he repeated his much, much better idea, he could then decide which he enjoyed more: the sound of bones breaking or the scream of intense fiery pain. Both now coming from the victim enlivened him! More than anything else in the world!

He grabbed Chuck's left arm, pulling, twisting and—

Thwack!

From above him, Ken dropped on top of the killer.

Taken by surprise, the killer dropped Chuck's left arm and managed to throw off Ken, who sent his snapping kicking foot slamming into the killer's throat.

The killer gasped for breath!

Like a shot, he flew up the stairs, out of Ken's grasp.

Ken quickly checked his partner and friend. Little he could do for Chuck now. Later.

He ran toward the steps and now, more certain of his footing, shot up the staircase that led to an office complex, long since abandoned.

And once again, total silence!

Not to be denied his revenge for Kelly, for his master, for what had just been done to his partner, and determined to save his wife and daughter from the death-dealing grasp of this maniac, Ken moved toward the office complex.

Two steps and a door to a small office swung open, slowly.

"Come closer, Detective . O'Hara," the killer taunted as the door swung open.

Ken moved toward the swinging door and saw inside, tied to a chair, gagged and blindfolded, Megan and Lauren.

"Far enough," the killer warned. "I have placed a crude bomb next to your wife and daughter. We have fifteen minutes for the Grand Championship match. Their life or death—it's in your hands." The killer pressed a button on a timer. The digital red letters began counting down. "There's no going back now," the killer laughed. "Shall we begin?"

"Leave my wife and daughter go!" Ken ordered.

"Go?" the killer sounded as if he couldn't believe his ears.

"They are nothing to you!" Ken shouted.

"Exactly," the killer sneered, "but they are everything to you. Now," he stuck one of his metal rod fingers into Ken's chest, "you have the motivation to fight me with everything you have. You are like the samurai," the killer was enthused, adding, "ready to die."

"I hope you're ready to die, motherfucker!" Ken corrected him, lifting and shoot his leg high into the air, whirling and sending his snapping foot into the killer's temple.

The killer reacted: feigning pain, dropping to the floor, then thrusting himself upward. His entire body slammed Ken up against the wall.

Against the wall, Ken threw an elbow to the killer's face. The killer backed off, spun and leaped, another snapping kick slamming Ken back up against the wall. Hard.

"I still haven't met my match!" the killer spat into Ken's face.

Ken back-handed the killer in the throat.

"You're going to meet your maker," he sneered at this psycho.

"Not today!" The killer whirled into the air, leaping beyond Ken's grasp.

Ken, fired with determination to save his wife and daughter, charged toward the killer, who himself charged with the thrill of finally meeting the mindhunter one-on-one; meeting the mindhunter only to find out the mindhunter's a wuss!

What a shame.

Maybe he should end it before the timer sent them all into kingdom come!

Less than five minutes remaining; the red numbers ticking down, burning into Ken's mind urgency.

"You couldn't save Kelly," the killer sneered. "You couldn't save your partner," the killer snickered. "And now," he glanced at the timer—4:20 to go—"you can't save your family!" He saw Ken's anger building, saw the detective trying to focus his entire being on him. "Or yourself!"

Suddenly, his laugh was everywhere again as the killer leaped into the air, whirling around and around like a dervish, thrusting out his two metal fingers toward Ken's eyes. He jabbed the metal spears toward Ken, who ducked, rolled, jumped up and, with everything in him, rammed his foot into the killer's lower back.

3:45 to go.

Ken slammed his foot into the killer's kidneys! The killer flew forward, smacking into the wall, cursing!

3:25 remaining.

The killer turned himself around the split second Ken's foot smashed into his jaw. The sound of cracking, breaking bone! His! The killer screamed in horror! His favorite thrilling sound was turning on him!

The red numbers read "1:45."

The killer ran toward the staircase. Ken grabbed the monster by the ankles, pulled him backward, down the steps, the killer's head smacking against each of the wooden steps.

"Nowhere to run, asshole!" Ken shot his foot into the base of the killer's neck. The killer's head bounced off the bottom step.

Then total silence.

With less than one minute remaining, Ken raced toward his wife and daughter. Megan, scared beyond belief, shook her head, trying to get Ken to understand. No time! No time!

With a lightning speed driven by deep love, Ken pulled the ropes off his wife and daughter, grabbed them both, pushing with all his might in the direction he thought was the door leading out. The three ran!

Ken rushed over to his fallen partner, slid his hands and arms underneath the unconscious cop, and lifted just as—

The bomb exploded!

Silver confetti flew everywhere! Millions and millions of silver slivers showering down upon Ken, Chuck, Megan and Lauren, followed by a metallic-sounding voice coming from somewhere.

"I am not a child killer, O'Hara."

And with that, Ken—his partner in his arms—moved toward Megan and Lauren.

"Let's go home, baby."

"Home?" Lauren asked, hoping.

Her father nodded.

"Home."

"For always?" Lauren's tiny voice sounded as if her father's answer was too hopeful to be true.

"Forever!"

Bloodmoon:
The Movie

The screenplay for *Bloodmoon* was produced at Carolco Studios (now Screen Gems) in Wilmington, NC. Keith Strandberg's previous credits include the following feature films:

No Retreat No Surrender (with Jean Claude Van Damme)

No Retreat No Surrender 2: Raging Thunder (with Cynthia Rothrock)

No Retreat No Surrender 3: Blood Brothers (with Joe Campanella, Keith Vitali)

The King of the Kickboxers (with Billy Blanks, Keith Cooke, Don Stroud, Richard Jaekel)

American Shaolin (with Cliff Lenderman)

SuperFights (with Keith Vitali, Cliff Lenderman, Chuck Jeffreys, Kelly Gallant)

The Screenplay
for Bloodmoon

Bloodmoon was conceived and begun approximately six years ago. After a meeting with Ng See Yuen, the president of Seasonal Film Corp., to discuss producing a big budget action feature showcasing today's best martial arts/action talent, Keith Strandberg thought of the project he was working on, a story that allowed for fantastic stunts and roles by experts in the martial arts.

After completing the writing, which included exhaustive research into serial killers and mindhinters, the cops who track them-the title was found: Bloodmoon. It refers to an old belief that a blood red moon at night means that someone will die violently. In the movie, many people do-at the hands of a deranged serial killer.

Now the search was on for stars. Gary Daniels was approached and secured for the lead role. Chuck Jeffreys, probably the most talented on-screen fighter and a wonderful actor, was signed for the co-lead. All that was left was to cast the rest of the roles, find all the locations, hire all the crew and make the movie.

Even though the script is set in New York, Wilmington, NC, was chosen because of the Carolco Studios facility. A great deal of inside filming was done there and the New York City back lot added a great deal of production value to the picture. Three days of second unit, exterior work in New York was also done to place the picture there.

Pre-production-the period when people are hired, locations are secured, equipment is rented etc.-began on April 15, 1996, and production started on May 20, 1996. The film was shot for 38 days-six days a week, averaging between 13 and 15 hours a day. It was a reasonably smooth shoot, due mainly to the fantastic cast, a very professional crew and great weather. Luckily, the first hurricane of the season didn't hit Wilmington until *after* the filming was completed.

Fight Scenes:

The hallmark of the action movies Keith Strandberg makes is the high quality of the fighting. The director, Tony Leung, was brought up in the same system as Jackie Chan, Samo Hung and Corey Yuen: the Chinese Opera training school. Tony is a contemporary of these great talents, and is taking his place among them. He was a finalist for a Golden Horse Award (the Asian equivalent of the Academy Awards) for action direction and choreography, and he is one of the founders and the current President of the Hong Kong Stuntman's Association. He is also a member of the Hong Kong Director's Guild, and has become a key player in the Hong Kong film industry.

Tony Leung knows action better than anyone else, and all that really had to be done was to find the best fighters, train them to fight for the cameras, then turn him loose. Some of the great fighters cast include: former three-time national champion Keith Vitali, former heavyweight champion of the world Joe Hess, living legend

Joe Lewis, WMAC Master Hakim Alston, professional wrestler Rob Van Dam, and Hall of Famer Michael DePasquale, Jr., among others. Many newcomers were also given their first breaks as fighters.

Much care-and time-are taken with the fight scenes, and they are filmed until they are right. Tony Leung won't settle for anything less than perfection, and sometimes that means 30 or 40 takes of the same sequence of moves. It's demanding for the actors and fighters, but excellence is the goal, and excellence is in the details.

Fight scenes are the life blood of a martial arts action movie. If you rented a martial arts movie and there weren't any fight scenes, you'd feel cheated. For all the attention and detail paid to the story, dialogue and the other elements of a film project, the bottom line is that a martial arts action picture lives or dies on the fights.

If the fights are good, the picture usually does well (assuming that the rest of the picture is up to snuff). But if the fight scenes are poorly executed, the film has less chance to succeed.

There are some notable exceptions to this, however. *The Karate Kid* is one. Though the movie was well done, the fight scenes were not—at least not from a martial arts standpoint. It was very easy to tell that none of the major actors had had any martial arts training. Lead actor Ralph Macchio is painfully bad as a fighter, but tremendous as an actor.

But, *The Karate Kid* was not really a martial arts movie: it was more of a mainstream movie that was set in the martial arts. And they cast the movie with that in mind. They weren't necessarily looking for fighters; they were looking for actors first, and they faked the action.

Real fighting and movie fighting are two completely different animals. What looks good on screen, and what works in the street are miles apart. Bruce Lee, that movie icon who made his living by kicking people in the head in his films, once remarked that in a real situation, he'd never go for the head. It's too small, he said, and too hard to hit. He'd go for the leg or the groin, instead. Well, why don't you do that on film? he was asked. Because it wouldn't look as good, he replied.

And he was right.

Fighting on the screen is designed to be entertainment, and those that have tried to make fight scenes realistic have been rewarded with cinematic failure. When an actor throws an opponent to the ground, it's not very dramatic. But, when an actor jumps 5 feet in the air and spin kicks the bad guy in the face, whipping his head around and sending him down three flights of stairs, it's...well, you get the idea.

So, Are The Actors Really Hitting Each Other or What?

Technically, they aren't supposed to hit each other, but often they end up doing just that. Actors are a considerable investment for a production company. With Stallone making upwards of $20 million a picture, who's going to hit him in the face? The producers cringe every time a punch comes too close, or pain screws up those beautiful, and expensive, features. Having a star injured means expensive down time, which in some big budget pictures can be as much as $100,000 to $500,000 a day.

The stars are not supposed to be throwing or taking the punches. That is why, in most big budget pictures, and most TV shows, they use professional stunt men.

In lower budget pictures, or movies that use real fighters, stunt men aren't normally used, and they let the actors and actresses fight it out. The thinking is, if the actors are fighters, they ought to be used to the pain, and they'll get over it.

How can you tell if the movie you are watching is using stunt people instead of the stars? If you can see the actors' faces during a fight scene, they aren't using stunt doubles. If for most of the action, including the difficult bits, all you see of the star is his back, *Bingo*— stunt double! For most of the action in the film *Beverly Hills Cop*, for example, Eddie Murphy is doubled— probably by order of the producer. On the flip side of that, one of the kings of martial arts movies, Jackie Chan, refuses to use a stunt double-ever. And, it has cost him— he injured his head very badly in a fall, and spent more than a month in the hospital, and has had a host of other injuries.

Even when the actors are really the ones fighting, the agreement is that there should be no contact to the face, and only light contact to the body. But, mistakes do happen.

On the set of *No Retreat No Surrender*, martial arts star Jean Claude Van Damme (*Bloodsport*, *Kickboxer*, *Double Impact*, etc.) was supposed to jump crescent kick Pete "Sugarfoot" Cunningham (a real life world champion kick boxer), as he rushed across the set, barely missing him.

When the director called "action", Van Damme jumped and kicked Pete right in the face, knocking him out immediately. Pete, a middleweight champion, fell to the ground like a stone, and Van Damme finished the shot without pausing to see if he was OK—which is exactly what you are supposed to do.

You see, if you do make contact, and then stop in the middle, before the director calls "cut", you won't just hurt your fellow actor, you'll ruin the shot. And that means you'll have to do it again.

As it was, Van Damme had to do the scene again, just for insurance, in case something was wrong with the first shot, and he hit Pete again, though he didn't knock him out this time. It turned out that the first shot was good, and that was the one that ended up in the movie. It looks realistic, and painful—which it certainly was.

From a production standpoint, one of the hardest things to do is to see a man get hit hard during a fight scene, and not break concentration before the director says "cut". But you have to wait until the director ends a scene before you rush into the shot and wipe up the blood.

Keith Vitali, a veteran martial arts actor (*Revenge of the Ninja, No Retreat No Surrender 3: Blood Brothers, American Kickboxer 1, SuperFights* and *Bloodmoon)* and former 3 time National Karate Champion, tells a story from his making of "Meals on Wheels" in Spain. "The director, Samo Hung, and the star, Jackie Chan, were good friends, but they had a natural rivalry," Vitali explains. "There was a scene where I had to kick Jackie in the chest with my side kick. Now, my side kick is my trademark, my most powerful kick, and as we were going through the scene, I was hitting him pretty hard, but Samo kept asking for 'More Power!' So, I hit him harder, and Jackie kept dropping to the ground, cringing and crying, then Samo would call for us to do it again. I hit Jackie so hard I thought I was going to kill him! Samo thought it was great fun!"

The Stunts:

Bloodmoon was also a stunt-heavy movie. There were some high falls, several explosions, a motorcycle slide, even a gag with a cargo net hung 100 feet over hard and unforgiving concrete. The best stunt coordinators and stunt men were hired, and everything went off without a hitch. No one got hurt, and the footage looks fantastic.

It's interesting the way different people perceive things. In Hong Kong, where Tony Leung does most of his work, a high fall isn't a very big deal. It's done all the time, and no one gets particularly excited about it. They take the proper safety precautions, but no one gets overly concerned. It's fairly routine.

In the US, and especially in Wilmington (Brandon Lee died on the Carolco lot, remember), things are much different. Maybe it's because stunts are not so routine, or Americans are much more apt to be concerned and excited, but every little stunt (even something as simple as going out a candy glass window) is a major deal. It got to be kind of a joke on the set between the producer and the Hong Kong side of the crew when people began strutting around, working themselves all up about a stunt that to the people performing it was boringly routine and very, very safe.

The stunts in *Bloodmoon* are phenomenal and add a new, fantastic element to what was already a very exciting, action packed movie.

The Cast of
Bloodmoon:

Gary Daniels is the lead, Ken O'Hara. He has made more than twenty action movies. Gary is becoming a star in action movies, and has a real opportunity to become very big, very hot. He's got all the right elements: movie star looks, a great, muscular body, good acting skills, and phenomenal martial arts ability. He is also fearless and did most of his stunts on *Bloodmoon* While filming the fight at the Forge, the actors were on a small walkway that was bounded by a 110' fall on one side. Tony wanted Gary to do a jump spinning side kick, and every time he did, he bumped against a flimsy railing! Gary wasn't troubled at all by it. In fact, he seemed to enjoy it!

Chuck Jeffreys plays Gary's partner Chuck is a 15 year veteran of martial arts movies. He is also a stunt man who has doubled Wesley Snipes, Eddie Murphy and many other well known actors. Chuck is one of the best martial artists around, and his fighting ability on the screen is phenomenal. He has the most talent of anyone out there, and is destined to be a huge star. Chuck has an unusual sense of humor, and it was his idea to add the line, "Unless you're growing, you better sit your ass down!" to the drug dealer fight scene.

Darren Shahlavi is a relative newcomer, but he has a very bright future. An extremely talented actor and a phenomenally hard worker, Darren has made a couple of Hong Kong movies, but *Bloodmoon* was his first American picture. A great kicker and a flamboyant fighter, Darren can do just about anything. And, with Tony Leung as the director, that's just what happened!

Frank Gorshin plays the Chief of Police, Chief Hutchins. Frank's most famous role was "The Riddler" on the TV *series Batman*. Frank is a great actor, and a fun guy. Frank was one of the original stand up comedians, and he's a riot to be around.

Jeff Pillars plays the role of Justice, the computer hacker. Jeff is an up and coming actor from the South, who had a big role in the CBS movie *The Stepford Wives*. During the filming the scene inside Justice's apartment, Jeff and fellow actors were hard pressed to keep straight faces. Not only were the adult themed props distracting everyone, but the actors kept cracking each other up. They got through the scene-just barely.

Joe Hess is a former world heavyweight champion, and he is a bear of a man. In spite of his 6'3" and 320+ pound frame, Joe is one of the nicest guys in the business. He is also a fantastic martial artist and accomplished stunt man (he's worked with just about everyone, from Don Johnson on *Miami Vice* to Kevin Costner in *The Bodyguard*).

Keith Vitali, a three time world champion and one

of the top ten fighters of all time, also served as the co-producer of the film. Keith's primary responsibility was casting, focusing on the fighters and the featured extras once the principal cast was in place. Keith also filled in as a fighter in a fight scene on the beach. Keith had the arduous task of auditioning the exotic dancers and the bikini-clad actresses we needed for the movie. A tough job, but somebody had to do it.

That, in a nutshell, is some insight into the movie, *Bloodmoon*

Remember: "There's blood on the moon tonight."

A blood red moon—a "Bloodmoon"—means one thing: someone is going to die violently. And bloodmoons are appearing far too often over the city of New York.

A lunatic mass murderer is stalking and killing the strongest victims he can find—martial artists who have proven themselves in the ring. But now they fight to the death.

To track down the murderer the NYPD must bring in a "Mindhunter"—a serial killer specialist. He is their only hope of stopping the carnage before the next…

BLOODMOON

BY

CARTER JOHNSON

ADAPTED FROM THE SCREENPLAY BY

KEITH W. STRANDBERG
